Matthew Everett

ISBN: 978-1-922565-59-4
Published by Vivid Publishing
A division of Fontaine Publishing Group
P.O. Box 948, Fremantle
Western Australia 6959
www.vividpublishing.com.au

A catalogue record for this
book is available from the
National Library of Australia

Cover art and illustrations by Tia Le Cerf

About the Author

Matthew C Everett was born in 1976 and raised in Crystal Brook, South Australia.

Growing up on the family farm afforded him many opportunities to be creative and this spawned his love of gardening, conservation and writing.

As an Education Consultant and a gardener of thirty-five years thus far, he enjoys advocating on animal and environmental issues, candle making and keeping fit.

He supports the work of various community groups including WWF, The Humane Society and Trees for Life.

This is Matt's first novella in the paranormal mystery genre.

Melt

When the fire within, incinerates your soul

For Nan

Without her encouragement, interest, gentle prodding, keen
eye and love, none of this would have been possible.

Lotsa love xx

Contents

Constance

Lightning crackled across the horizon, as dark thunderous storm clouds forced their way over the hills of Salem Village, Massachusetts. As the winds intensified, trees flexed and groaned, casting off debris. Animals stirred with nervous excitement as the temperature plummeted. Citizens, doing their best to hold onto their hats and remain upright against the force of the wind, scurried like ants frantically preparing for the worst.

Meanwhile, inside the large, ornate courthouse, a storm of a different kind was brewing as the trial against Constance Lucille Martinez drew to its inevitable conclusion. The judge, John Winthrop Ellis, demanded silence in his courtroom as his hand-carved, hickory gavel hit the large solid oak desk several times.

Constance Martinez was a slender, beautiful young wife and mother with a toddler and a newborn to care for. As part of her care, and to help with healing and general wellbeing, the local herbalist had encouraged her to mix and consume a tonic, twice daily. Dutifully following the advice, she prepared each tonic and her health gradually improved. One morning, in a cruel and calculated twist, her neighbour, Miss Sylvia Strathmont, overheard Constance reading aloud the ingredients. This led to her being accused of practising witchcraft.

As it was for the time, an accusation alone was justification to commence a hearing in front of a judge and jury of her peers. Sylvia, the granddaughter of the town herbalist, was secretly in love with Constance's husband. She used the witchcraft trials as a means to have the community remove the obstacle in her way. She had nothing against Constance; she just wanted what Constance possessed. As she took the stand to give her embellished version of events, the wind raged outside, whistling through the rafters and eaves like a chorus of wailing Banshees. The storm's noisy intrusion smothered the occasional whimper from Constance's newborn daughter.

Earlier, through streaming tears, Constance had pleaded for her life, stating her case as eloquently as an uneducated woman could. Her husband sat ashen-faced in the public gallery, knowing the truth rarely mattered in these cases. The hysteria, paranoia and the sway of public opinion, far outweighed it. Though generally docile and submissive, Constance was known to be opinionated. Even so, she believed herself to be well liked and trusted within the community, and through her husband's business connections. However, as she fought for her life against the flawed, corrupt process, there was nothing her husband could do to help. He feared he was already tainted by association. The community had endured so much angst and pain as a result of the trials and speaking in Constance's defence had put others in the cross-hairs of suspicion. As a result, many, including Constance's husband, chose to remain silent to save themselves. Constance suspected this and didn't hold it against him. He was a good, fair and gentle man, and she needed him to take care of their two beautiful children. Even if, by some miracle, she was found innocent, she knew the stigma that would plague her family in the years ahead, would be a heavy burden.

The discussion amongst the jurors didn't take long. In just over half an hour they announced their guilty verdict. At that very moment, lightning struck the courthouse steeple, sending splinters of wood in all directions. As the current continued toward the ground it instantly claimed the life of the elected spokesman where he stood. A strong gust of wind flung open the heavy oak entrance doors and shattered several windows, scattering paperwork and people alike. Constance calmly stood. Her floor-length, black gown and long black hair appeared to move in slow motion compared to the manic scene around her. She glanced across at her deathly pale and now-distraught husband holding their two crying children and mouthed the words 'It will be alright',- before the bailiff led her away.

Outside the courtroom, as she was tied to a large wooden stake atop her judgment pyre, she raised her right arm and extended her index finger towards the judge. Shouting above the wind and the jeers of the few who had stayed after the verdict, she cursed every female born of his line. She stated they would all die at the hands of fire in their third decade of life. The judge, standing defiant next to the bailiff, winced as he heard her statement, before instructing the others to light the pyre.

Although it had been raining heavily, the fuel ignited

instantly. Shielding himself and the children from the inclement weather, her grief-stricken husband stared out one of the shattered courtroom windows, attempting to catch a final glimpse of his wife's beautiful face. She must have sensed his longing, because she turned her head towards him, returned a slivered smile, and then looked silently towards the heavens as the flames engulfed her.

For those who heard her statement that day, it was a vindication of the verdict. For those to come, the legacy of her wrath would impose unimaginable suffering and premature death.

John Winthrop Ellis was deeply saddened by the witch trials, as he, too, was a pawn in the game, having to play his role. He was acutely aware the community would judge him for his decisions. He knew his legacy would be irreparably scarred. However, it was his distinct lack of understanding for the supernatural that caused him to underestimate the judgment that would be inflicted upon him and his descendants.

* * *

As upsetting as it was to see Constance burned to death, based largely on her embellished testimony, Sylvia also felt a twisted sense of relief. In her own mind, her path to happiness was now clear. She was attractive, smart, bright and blonde — attributes she knew would provide a solid foundation upon which to build a relationship with the right man. She would offer her sympathy to Constance's husband in the days and weeks ahead and would make herself available to him for whatever he needed to ease his grief. She had possessive eyes only for him.

The bad weather had abated, and apart from the damage to the courthouse from the lightning strike, the rest of the town seemed to have escaped serious harm. Sylvia returned to the herbalist shop, where she occasionally worked, to find the front window smashed and the front door ajar.

'Hello? Is anyone there? Genevieve?'

Genevieve was a portly, middle-aged widow, with a kind, round face and shoulder-length salt and pepper hair. The kind of grandmother figure every child wished they had. She was also the town herbalist. Sylvia knew she was currently away trading supplies in the next town, but instinctively called her name nevertheless. She was certain she had locked the front door upon leaving the shop earlier that day to head to the courthouse. As she entered and navigated her way past the broken glass on the floor, she removed her soggy cape, which had kept her long woollen dress mostly dry, and hung it alongside her linen cap on a hook near the door. Grabbing a broom, she began to clean up. Looking around the shop, nothing seemed to be out of place or missing; however, a chill in the air unsettled her.

After several hours of restorative work, Sylvia set a pot to boil on the combustion stove and located the herbal tea. As she stepped out of the room to get changed, a strong gust caused some glass bottles to rattle and fall over on a shelf above the table, dislodging the corks and spilling their contents. After a moment, and ignoring the mess, Sylvia returned to pour her tea and allowed it to steep while she plated some course bread and a slice of fruit pie.

Within half an hour of consuming her hastily prepared refreshments, she began to experience blurred vision. Instinctively shaking her head and rubbing her eyes didn't seem to help. As she stood and made her way to the wash pale on the bench, she was overcome by dizziness and severe nausea. Reaching out for something to grab a hold of, she steadied herself between the table and the bench. Fearing she had consumed something other than herbal tea, she searched frantically for the tin. Struggling to read the label as her eyes refused to focus, a moment of clarity between worsening symptoms gave relief as she established it was, indeed, herbal tea. The reprieve was brief, as the onset of a strong headache resulted in loss of balance and she collapsed on the floor. Writhing in pain, she curled up as stomach pains set in.

By now, Sylvia knew she had been poisoned, but she had no idea how or with what. Her throat constricted as a convulsion took over, resulting in foaming at the mouth and an inability to speak. After a few minutes, as the convulsion subsided, Sylvia lay temporarily motionless and exhausted, clinging to life with shallow, rapid breaths. It was too late. She hadn't paid attention to the debris on the table or pieced together the symptoms quickly enough to source an antidote. A shadowy figure, observing the commotion from a darkened corner of the shop, proceeded to glide toward her. Movement out the corner of her blood-shot and tear-filled eye drew Sylvia's attention, and she slowly turned her head. Her eyes widened, and the blood drained from her face, as the translucent shadow solidified and hovered over her.

'Your accusation caused my family to lose a wife and mother, all because you wanted what wasn't yours to take. I see the predicament you're in confuses. Allow me to enlighten you. Deadly Nightshade root powder and ground Oleander flower are both highly toxic when mixed together and in quantities larger than a pinch. If you hadn't been so absentminded when pouring your tea earlier, you might have noticed the contamination. Never mind. It's my turn to dispense justice and balance the ledger — a life for a life —,' Constance boomed in a scathing tone.

Petrified and struggling to move, Sylvia managed to turn her head towards the shop door and strained to look in the direction of the courthouse, where a sliver of smoke from the murderous bonfire was still visible. Constance Martinez's bones were still warm and yet, it appeared she had escaped the town's judgment entirely. Another convulsion took hold of what little breath Sylvia had left in her lungs, before a single, final tear ran down her cheek.

For the time being, the ledger was again balanced. The year was 1692.

Chapter One

Taken

Margaret Cynthia Ellis liked to have a drink each night to calm her nerves. She had suffered from anxiety most of her life, so her doctor recommended a brandy before bed whenever she felt she needed it. Whilst others found solace in religion, she found hers in the bottom of a bottle. She was fast approaching middle age, her surrogate farmer's wife existence etched so clearly on her prematurely lined face. The reflection she saw in the mirror wasn't the bright, youthful, happy-go-lucky one it once was. She could thank her anxiety and years of alcohol consumption for that. Her younger brother, William, had tragically lost his beautiful wife Bernadette only nine months prior, as a result of complications during the birth of their third child. Margaret was unmarried, so she had offered to move in to support him.

On this particular night, the extended family had come over for dinner. Her nieces, Eileen and Geraldine, were toddlers, gaily playing hide and go seek together. Henry, their younger brother, was in his cot, and William was in the kitchen. He had been chained to the combustion stove, dutifully preparing a roast, for the best part of the afternoon.

After several hours of indulging in good food, conversation and company, Margaret felt she needed an injection of courage and headed upstairs to sneak a brandy or two before returning to her guests and seeing the evening out. She'd hidden the bottle in the back of her bureau. It was her vice, and she indulged. After all, her doctor had endorsed it.

The carpeted floor was soft and inviting underfoot as she slipped her shoes off and placed them on the landing. She buried her toes in the long shagpile fibres which sent a pleasurable shiver up the length of her spine. The heat from the combustion stove made the air warm and comfortable, tantalising her nostrils with the scent of the earlier roast dinner. Making her way towards the bureau, she removed her lemon-coloured bolero cardigan and threw it on the bed, before retrieving the brandy bottle and glass from their hiding place.

Seated at her dressing table staring into the mirror, she studied her thick, brunette, shoulder-length hair as she drank. The greys seemed to be multiplying and she made a mental note to book a hairdressing appointment for the following week. As she poured her third glass, she ran her fingers through her hair, only to pause when she noticed a translucent blue flash enter her left ear. She felt no pain but was instantly paralysed.

* * *

Downstairs, William noticed the light in the dining room dim and flicker, as his dinner guests prepared to leave. Each in turn shouted out to Margaret upon their departure. They were aware she liked to sneak away for a tipple and figured she had just fallen asleep on the bed after doing so.

As the last of the guests left, William called out to

Margaret, but there was no answer. As he began to ascend the stairs, his muscular frame, sculpted from years of physical labour, was revealed as he removed his blazer jacket and laid it to rest on the ornate newel post at the top of the staircase. He first noticed her shoes, neatly sitting side by side outside her bedroom door. He reached for the metal doorknob, only to recoil. It was unusually hot to touch. He tried again using his handkerchief, brushing it off as a consequence of having had the combustion fire burning for longer than usual to cook the roast. He knocked before pushing the bedroom door open. There was no answer. An immediate bluish-grey haze was visible in the air which smelled smoky-sweet but rancid. Again, though this puzzled him, he dismissed it. The flue for the combustion stove ran up through the floor in the corner, then out through the ceiling. It could have allowed some smoke into the room, as it had been a while since it had been thoroughly cleaned.

The bed was undisturbed. The light in the bedroom was on but very dim. When he looked up he noticed the bulb had partially melted and was covered in a black substance he deemed to be soot. Touching the bedpost to get a better look at the bulb, his hand slipped. In the dim light, his eyes took a moment to focus as he looked down at his hand. It was covered with a sticky, yellowish, fat-like substance. Rational thought had by now gone out the window, because nothing he was seeing made any sense. *I've used the combustion stove many times to prepare a roast in the past without this kind of internal pollution.*

Turning to his left, he noticed the bureau drawer was ajar. It was then he saw what remained of his sister's body, still smouldering in the corner.

Staggering backwards, he hit the wall. Instant nausea overcame him, and he vomited his earlier roast dinner all over his shoes.

'God damn it all,' he cursed.

After several moments, he slowly regained his composure, propped himself up against the bureau, and continued to take in the gruesome and repulsive scene. His eyes and brain were unable to reconcile the devastation he was seeing. He grabbed his handkerchief from his pants pocket. After wiping his mouth, he used it to cover his nose in a vain attempt to cease breathing in his sister's deathly aroma.

Her blackened, but otherwise complete left hand was clenched around the empty and still-intact brandy glass. It was all that remained of her left arm. Her skull lay next to it, noticeably shrunken and denuded of all skin and hair. It was right side down, as if she had fallen asleep with her head resting on the dresser. Her left leg had detached from the pelvic bone, which had mostly disintegrated and lay prostrate on the floor. It was still smouldering from the hip joint but was otherwise unaffected by whatever had happened. Her right leg had fused to the antique glass, ball and claw adjustable stool she had been sitting on and, again, was otherwise unburned from the knee down. The padding on the stool had melted away to the circular metal base plate beneath. There was no visible evidence of her torso, spine or right arm, just what appeared to be a yellowish, wet-looking, ash pile around the base of the stool.

The mirror on the dresser had cracked and blackened but was otherwise intact, as was much of the dresser itself. Being wooden, it seemed odd it hadn't been consumed by the apparent fire. A mustard-coloured, dresser lamp with ruffled shade, a mere two feet from her remains, appeared in pristine condition. It was functioning, the bulb hadn't melted, and it looked as though it had been placed in the room after the fire had extinguished. At the base of the lamp, he noted her favourite wooden-handled hairbrush, with undamaged bristles and unsinged hair embedded in it. Immediately next to it was her signature scarlet lipstick which had completely melted into a glossy pool.

Why didn't she scream? The scorch marks around her body were minimal and quite contained. The fire had burned very hot, very quickly and then extinguished. Only the carpet directly beneath her chair had burned through to the boards beneath. The wall above the dresser was scorched all the way up to the ceiling, and the old paintwork had bubbled and peeled away in places. The empty brandy bottle, lying on its side, was just visible, partially covered by the ash pile at the base of the stool.

The reality of what had taken place started to emotionally incapacitate him. Upon exiting the room, his breathing laboured and he felt weak and tingly. Shock and grief took over, causing him to collapse to the floor, thoroughly distraught. After several moments, his daughter, Eileen, sat next to him on the landing and placed her hand on top of his.

'Daddy, why are you crying? Where's Aunty Margie?' She asked, softly and innocently.

When their eyes met, he managed a smile, pulled her close and gave her a reassuring hug. He had no words to answer either question. Gathering his thoughts, he picked her up, closed the bedroom door and descended the stairs. His life, and that of his children, had again been plunged into the depths of despair. He hoped they would be too young to understand the tragedy that had taken Aunty Margie from them at just thirty-four years of age. He had an urgent phone call to make. As he dialled the police, he glanced at his pocket watch and noted that, from the time she had excused herself to head upstairs, to when he'd found her body, only one and a half hours had lapsed.

It was spring of 1936, in Louisville, Alabama, and it would be remembered for all the wrong reasons.

Chapter Two

Heavenish

Margaret became acutely aware, after waking abruptly, that she was moving at speed. At least that was the sensation she felt; although she wasn't on or inside any discernible vehicle. Upon opening her eyes, everything was opaque, which caused her to instinctively rub them, thinking she had blurred vision. That wasn't the problem. As suddenly as she had woken, the sensation of movement stopped, and she got up from the seated position she found herself in.

Am I hallucinating? Is this a dream?

She gently slapped both sides of her face. The only familiarity in that moment was the burned rags resembling clothes she'd been wearing … the night she died. Shapes moved about her that were human-like, but had no discernible features. They wore non-descript, oversized white robes. Apart from the seemingly non-existent wings, they could almost have been angels. Her voice sounded muffled as she tried to call out. Without any idea of where she was heading, Margaret began to walk down a wide, windowless corridor and was joined by several others who looked equally as lost and confused. Nobody spoke. She deemed them to be new arrivals, like her, as they appeared human, and were dressed in everyday clothing.

'Margaret Ellis?'

The female voice stopped her dead in her tracks. It was familiar, but couldn't be who she was thinking about. She turned.

'Bernadette? Oh my God, it's really you. But, how can that be, unless I'm –.'

'We'll get to all that. It's nice to see you. Although, I was hoping it would be longer before I did.' Bernadette interrupted, as they hugged each other.

'So, I am dead then? What is this place? Is it heaven?' Margaret asked on a single breath.

'Okay, okay. I know this is a lot to take in. I remember feeling the same when I first arrived. Let's take a seat.'

'Okay, sure, but where? There aren't any.' Margaret looked in every direction seeing nothing but white space.

'Trust me. Just sit.' Bernadette said, and as she did so, the white space supported her weight.

Hesitantly, Margaret followed suit and felt the space cushion her. Waving her arm beneath her bottom, she struggled to grasp that she was literally sitting on air. 'Remarkable, so what is this place?'

'Let me start by answering your earlier questions,' Bernadette said, as she reached over and took Margaret's hands. 'You aren't dreaming and, yes, you have died. This place is probably best described as a waiting room. My understanding is that it isn't heaven. I call it Heavenish.'

From the corner of her eye, over Bernadette's left shoulder, Margaret saw a dark, ominous shadow zip past.

'What on earth was that?'

'Ah, yes. I need to tell you about that. New arrivals have to undergo an assessment. It usually happens when you're in a resting state, as there's no need for sleep here. It can happen at any time and you almost don't know it's happening. I say almost, as it feels as though your insides are being rearranged, which is a little unpleasant. It only happens once. Don't be afraid.'

'An assessment? By whom and for what?'

'The black shadow you see from time to time is called a soul wraith. They do the assessments to check if you're pure of heart.'

'How do I know if I'm pure of heart?' Margaret asked, tensing as another wraith passed close by.

'If you're not taken, then you are.'

'Taken?'

'Yes, they go to another place and aren't seen again.'

'Let's hope I'm not taken then.'

'Indeed.'

'Have you been here the whole time, or did you know I was expected and came to meet me?'

'Both. I want to thank you for taking care of my family. I was most concerned how William would cope when I left. My soul relaxed when you moved in –.'

A wraith materialised right next to Margaret, and Bernadette stood and retreated obediently. Margaret was in a trance-like state as the wraith hovered around her for just a few seconds. It was all the time needed to complete a thorough assessment, before the wraith left in search of the next new arrival. Bernadette returned, and with a gentle touch on her forearm, Margaret was released from her trance-like state. She felt a little agitated and slightly confused as she clutched and rubbed at her mid-section whilst tugging at her clothes, checking to see if anything was missing.

'I'm sorry. I must have zoned out there for a second. What were we discussing?'

'It's okay. You were just assessed, and you've passed, otherwise we wouldn't be talking right now. I wanted to get it out of the way early and knew it would happen whilst we were relaxed and seated,' Bernadette admitted.

'Phew. I wasn't taken. I have so many questions and yet I feel like I already know the answers. How is that possible?'

'I call it the upload. It happens during your assessment. It's almost as if everything you ever wondered when you were alive is suddenly explained or revealed without having to ask the questions.'

'That's fantastic. Do you know why you're still here? What I mean is, you died nine months ago and yet you're still here rather than being … in heaven.'

'Time is meaningless here. It isn't linear or chronological like our understanding when we were alive. There is no day or night. No clocks or watches to refer to. No birthdays or anniversaries to celebrate. When I received my upload, I knew I was to remain here until the next member of my family arrived to be inducted.'

'So, you could literally disappear at any time then?'

Margaret said, concerned at the thought of being left alone in a strange place.

'Once the induction is complete, I could. I sense you're inquisitive about the opaque figures you can see around us –, why they look different and don't interact.'

Margaret nodded. 'They're angels in training, aren't they?'

'Yes. After a period of time, the new arrivals, who are pure of heart, transition into the realm of angels.'

We're going to be angels.

For all the issues Margaret had dealt with while she was alive, her pure love and devotion towards family had never wavered.

'Now, this might sound a little strange, but I want you to stare over my right shoulder and think of yourself sitting at my old dressing table, staring into the mirror.'

'Okay. What will I –'

'It will all become clear. Trust me.'

As both sat and Margaret complied, the dressing table appeared through the white abyss, and an image materialised in the mirror. At first, she didn't recognise who it was. She was young and vibrant, with thick, luscious auburn hair, and blemish-free skin that had a radiant healthy glow.

'Oh my God!' Margaret gasped. 'I'm sorry I didn't mean –' she looked up out of habit. 'Wow, it's me, and I'm young and wrinkle-free again.'

'You have been returned to the best and healthiest version of yourself.' Bernadette stood, turned side-on, to reveal her pre-baby svelte figure. She cupped her hands under her chin, fluttering her eyelids, they both laughed.

Another group of new arrivals materialised through the white abyss, looking anxious and confused. The array of attire they wore indicated who they were and where they'd found themselves in their last moments. As Margaret studied each of them, images flashed in her mind, like she was watching a movie, about how they died.

A woman in a damaged wedding dress, stood with a man in a suit, and several tattered bridesmaids and flower girls. They had all died in a multi-vehicular collision on their way to the church. The driver had swerved on a dirt road and lost control. He veered onto the wrong side and collided with an approaching grain truck. A minister and several parishioners, dressed in their Sunday best, were covered in blood stains. They had perished whilst praying when a woman opened fire at a mosque. An infant, wrapped in a new baby blanket, too young to crawl, was being carried by its mother. The baby had died suddenly in the night, and the mother, who'd had three miscarriages previously, was so distraught she'd taken an overdose. A totally naked, slim toned man was also amongst them. His nakedness didn't offend, nor was he self-conscious about his appearance. From the look on his face, 'stunned' would have been the best description. He'd died of a heart attack whilst having sex with his mistress. An elderly couple, walking hand in hand and just shy of their sixty-ninth wedding anniversary, had died hours apart, in separate rooms at the nursing home where they resided. A uniformed police officer was surprised by an intruder in the driveway of his home as he left for work. A struggle ensued, and he sustained a single, fatal bullet wound to the chest.

Margaret joined Bernadette, and both indicated the newcomers should continue in the direction they were loosely moving, to where any prior loved ones would meet them and initiate them into their new surrounds.

'Hey, Bernadette, you said something earlier I didn't quite catch onto, but now I'm inquisitive about it.'

'Oh, and what was that?'

'You said something about your soul relaxing when I moved in with William.'

'Yes, that's right. I did.'

'So, you could see from here that I had done that, and … Oh my God, everything?' Margaret was suddenly aware of the scope of her own question and felt a pang of self-consciousness.

'Yes, everything. It's not my place to judge anyone else. We're born flawed and we die flawed. Let me show you the viewing room.'

Bernadette indicated for Margaret to once again sit, and they joined hands.

'I want you to clear your mind of everything and focus only on William,' Bernadette said.

As Margaret relaxed, closed her eyes and did as she was instructed, the feeling of motion was again apparent. Suddenly, she found herself in the rafters of a packed church. William and the children were seated in the front row.

'Seriously? I'm at my own funeral? I get to see who turned up to see me off?'

Bernadette smiled.

'Do you know how many times over the years we discussed what it would be like to attend your own funeral?'

'I do. Eleven to be exact,' Bernadette quipped.

As they watched the service from their lofty vantage point, a pigeon flew up and settled next to them, seemingly unaware of their presence. Margaret felt emotional when she saw how upset William and the children were and wanted to reassure them she was okay.

'Can I just –.'

'No. Unauthorised interaction with the living isn't permitted. Grief is the price you pay for love and mustn't be denied. There will come a time, but it isn't today. We should go now,' Bernadette confirmed as they held hands and returned.

Ten years later ...

Chapter Three

Care

'**G**ood morning, sweetheart. Happy birthday!' William said, as he sat on the end of Eileen's bed holding a tray of oatmeal, toast, an apple and a glass of orange juice.

'Morning Dad.' She yawned and stretched as he placed the tray in front of her.

Before another word could be uttered, Geraldine and Henry came bursting into the room, both talking at once about her birthday present.

'I told you both to wait until she had at least eaten her breakfast,' William scolded, but he removed the tray and Eileen got out of bed to join her siblings at the window.

'Dad got you a horse!' Geraldine gushed, folding her arms as the pang of jealousy reared its head.

'Can I have a horse too?' Henry innocently enquired, tugging at Eileen's nightgown.

Tied to the front fence post, was the most beautiful creature Eileen had seen. His shiny black coat glistened in the morning light. As if sensing an audience, he looked toward the house, catching Eileen's eye. He shook his mane, before turning toward a bushel of hay resting against the fence. The bold white stripe down the centre of his face was his only contrasting colour.

'Oh Dad, really? He's really mine?'

'Yes, sweetheart, he is. Old Mr Cassidy next door is retiring off the land next month, and he knew you'd been taking riding lessons. He offered him to me for a very reasonable price. He hasn't been ridden for a while and needs to be reshoed first. As we don't have a stable to keep him in, he will stay at the Cassidy's until I build one.'

'Hey Dad, he looks like he stuck his head in a tin of white paint.' Henry laughed.

'Aww Dad, thank you so much. The best birthday present of all,' Eileen said, giving him a tight, genuine hug.

'Now, everybody out! Eileen, get back into bed and finish your breakfast,' William ordered.

As Eileen complied, and William shut the door behind him, she turned and retrieved a photo frame from next to her bed placing it in her lap.

'You'd be so proud of him, Mum. He's made it work, with the help of Nan and Pop, and we all turned out alright.'

Half an hour went by before Eileen entered the kitchen, throwing the apple to herself.

'I wondered why there was an apple on my breakfast tray. You know I don't like them. But I know someone who will.'

William smirked and ushered her out the door.

As Eileen approached the horse, bright red apple in hand, he smelled the gift he was about to receive, shook his mane and neighed.

'It's okay, boy. It's alright. Here ya go.' Eileen said, as he gently took the apple from her palm.

'I'm going to take great care of you. Your name will be Saintly Sapphire.'

* * *

Another ten years later …

'Are you nervous?' Eileen asked, as they approached William's front door.

'Nah. She'll be right.' Tomas replied, though the palm holding Eileen's hand was sweaty, and he ran the other through his hair continually.

'Right. Well, you might want to look in a mirror and tell yourself that, honey, as currently your face says exactly the opposite. It'll be fine. Dad loves you. Just be yourself.'

Eileen's words provided the reassurance he needed. His heart was racing, nervous tension was building in his gut. He'd gone over and over the conversation he wanted to have, even planned for contingencies should the answer be negative.

Eileen took charge and knocked on the door.

'Eileen, sweetheart. It's good to see you. Come in, come in.' William ushered them forward, and they kissed and hugged. 'Tomas, welcome. You look a little peaky. Are you alright?'

'Fine William, just fine. You know me, tough as an ox. Always something to be done, plenty to keep me busy. I'm a little tired, I guess …' Tomas was rambling, but Eileen saved him by grabbing his hand and leading him through to the kitchen.

William smiled and shook his head before closing the door.

'Breathe darling. You don't want to pass out on me. Take a seat, and I'll put the kettle on.'

'So, what's news with you two? How's the ranch?' William enquired as he joined them in the kitchen.

'The ranch is good, never better, actually. Eileen's good. The tractor needs a bit more attention but nothing I can't handle.' Tomas replied, still fussing with his hair.

'Ah. That's good to hear.'

Eileen placed a mug of coffee in front of each of them, along with a plate of shortbread, before she took a seat. Tomas grabbed the cup immediately, so his hands were occupied. He felt like a bird whose wings had gotten too wet when they touched the surface of the ocean and he was floundering.

'We do have some news actually, Dad, or should I say, Tomas does,' Eileen stated, placing her hand on his shoulder and giving it a gentle squeeze as she took the seat next to him.

'Uh, hmm, yes. Well, William, as you know, Eileen and I have been going steady for a while now and I feel I should make an honest woman out of her. I know our relationship has been solid, but you never quite know how someone might react when asked –.'

'Of course you have my blessing to marry her, Tomas. I'd be honoured to have you as my son-in-law,' William interjected, sparing Tomas the continued awkwardness he'd tied himself up in since walking through the door.

'Really? Phew. That's a relief. Hey, Eileen, he said yes.' Tomas reiterated as the nerves and tension evaporated and blood returned to his face.

'I know, darling. I heard.'

They all laughed, and the happy couple kissed.

* * *

Five years later ...

'Dinner's ready,' Eileen shouted from their front porch, holding her heavily pregnant, thirty-one-year-old physique against the door frame. It was late winter in 1961. Her husband, Tomas and farmhand Hosea, had been mending a tyre on their only working tractor in the front paddock all day, in preparation for seeding, and now, as the light faded over the horizon, it was time to admit defeat until morning.

Tomas and Eileen Hubbard had inherited their farmhouse, land and approximately four-hundred head of stock from his father, Tomas Hubbard Snr, three years earlier, after his body was found in the field one morning.

The night of his death, Tomas Snr had taken up and shotgun and a gas lamp from the stock shed, after hearing a cow, in calf, calling out in distress. It was just after dusk. Fresh spring leaves were torn from their branches and danced in sporadic patterns as the turbulent wind controlled them. Others raced along the ground like they had to be the first to cross an imaginary finish line. A lone coyote howled from the ridge observing all. He could smell his next meal long before he saw it. After forty years of tending the land, the sound of a coyote still sent shivers down Tomas' spine.

Part way across the paddock he lost his footing and

stumbled, dropping the gas lamp which shattered upon impact and could not be relit. He knew his property like the back of his hand, even in the dark, and continued to make his way towards the distressed animal. The wind was getting stronger and he knew it was dangerous to be out in the elements alone. Over the years he had managed to assist many pregnant cows to deliver their calves, and the circumstance he found himself in was no different. The problem now was he had no light by lamp or moon. If he stayed, there would be limits to what he could do. If he returned to the stock shed to retrieve another lamp, it was time neither the pregnant cow, nor the calf might have. As he reluctantly decided to head back towards the house, he heard a rumble in the distance, which he deemed to be thunder, and quickened his pace. He knew he didn't want to be out in the open with the potential threat of lightning around.

Before Tomas Snr could take another step, a horrible realisation swept over him. The rumble he heard moments earlier wasn't thunder but the herd stampeding, something had spooked them. The red wolf and coyote were prevalent at this time of year and both would take advantage of a potential free meal during calving season. The ground beneath his feet began to tremble.

Tomas Jnr had been asked to run errands in town that afternoon, and upon returning to the house, he noticed it was cold and dark and his father didn't appear to be present. He called out in the direction of the front paddock, but the howling wind hurtling towards him, drowned his cries.

Knowing it was calving season, he figured his father was out with the stock, but he was concerned, as the weather was turning rapidly and the truck was still at the house. When he made his way to the stock shed, he noticed the shotgun and one of the gas lamps were missing. He grabbed another lamp, lit it and headed out into the dark, continuing to call for his father but getting no reply.

Tomas Snr saw his son in the distance as the gas lamp illuminated his position. He yelled a single word, at the top of his lungs, in his son's direction, and then quieter to himself, *I love you son*.

Tomas Jnr stopped dead in his tracks as he heard his father's exclamation on the wind. He knew instantly he was powerless to help. Even if he were to get the truck and head out in his father's general direction, there probably wasn't time, and the stampeding herd wouldn't necessarily avoid colliding with the vehicle, potentially crushing him inside it.

As a child he'd witnessed the destruction caused by hungry cattle. The family dog, Rusty, was a boisterous, sandy-coloured, eighteen-month-old Kelpie puppy, undergoing obedience training when he was unable to avoid being crushed to death as two herds converged on a centralised feeding station. His father had tried to shield Tomas from seeing Rusty's remains after the herd had dispersed, but curiosity had gotten the better of him. What was seen couldn't be unseen. Rusty's death silently haunted Tomas for many years. He'd learned a hard lesson on the ranch at a young age, and it wasn't one he wished to repeat. His father had other working dogs in the years that followed, but never again did Tomas allow himself to get close to any of them.

There was nothing he could do until morning when there would be light to see and hopefully the bad weather had abated. He made his way back inside and sat dejected by the window, staring out into the darkness as the wind whistled through the eaves. His right heel tapping constantly as his restless leg moved involuntarily. The memory of Rusty was playing over and over in his mind. Tomas heard a single gunshot ring out. Several thoughts flooded his mind. Had his father put a cow or her calf out of its misery? Was it actually a gunshot he'd heard? Had his father spared himself being crushed to death by the herd? He prayed for his father's safe return as tears welled in his eyes. His spirit ached; he knew he was already grieving.

As dawn broke over the horizon, the first rays of sunshine streamed in through the window. Tomas Jnr abruptly stirred. He immediately called for his father, but again there was no reply. During the night he'd hoped his father had managed to avoid being trampled. He checked the bedroom and discovered the bed hadn't been slept in. He feared the worst.

He bolted out the front door in the direction he'd headed the night before. His fears were realised when he came across his father's battered and lifeless body. His anguished cry, as he dropped to his knees, shattered the silence and nearby birds took flight. The shotgun, mangled and broken, was next to him. From the condition of the body, it was impossible to tell if he'd taken his own life. There was, however, evidence of desecration. A coyote or red wolf had been in the vicinity.

Tomas Jnr, fighting his emotions, chose to believe, until he was otherwise informed, that his father had spared himself an agonising death from the animals he cared greatly for. A short distance away was the dead cow and her calf he'd tried to assist. Tomas Snr was only fifty-nine years old.

* * *

The dilapidated Hubbard farmhouse wasn't much to look at but held great sentimental value. There had been many bleak cropping years, with only a couple of favourable ones in recent times, so only the essentials would see any money spent on them, as income had been minimal. Built from Hickory by Tomas' great-grandfather in the mid 1800's, it consisted of five main rooms – two bedrooms, a small kitchen, a living area, and a bathroom/washhouse and it was now in dire need of repair. The basic wooden structure barely kept the rain out, the windows and doors so ill-fitting they offered scant protection in the mildest of windy weather. The wooden shingle roof often leaked requiring constant attention. The front steps had rot in them, though you could avoid falling through them as long as you knew where to tread. The rickety handrail was barely able to support itself, let alone the weight of a heavily pregnant woman seeking stability as she entered or exited the premises. The front porch was small, with two upholstered armchairs surrounding a little, hand-made, three-legged wooden table. The armchairs, looking more wooden than upholstered, were showing wear and tear, with several springs beginning to break through the fraying floral fabric. Heating for the premises was via a combustion stove cooktop along the kitchen-living room wall, with wood sourced from the surrounding farmland.

Tomas didn't regard himself as a handyman, but he had a flair for mechanics. It was a skill his father had encouraged and nurtured. Upon his father's death Tomas doubted his ability to carry the family legacy. He only had ten years' experience directly working on the property since leaving school, a relatively short period of time in the life of a rancher. There were many aspects of his father's forty years on the land he simply didn't know enough about. Tomas Snr ran a tight ship when it came to managing the various responsibilities ranching demanded and would only hand them over to his son when he deemed he was ready. His father's colleagues and his father-in-law, William, had given much support in the months after Tomas Senior's death, educating him further on how to raise and manage cattle, crop rotation procedures and balancing the books. This proved invaluable for Tomas Jnr when he was promoted to Manager, before his time, at twenty-eight years of age.

The ranching lifestyle agreed with Tomas' need to burn off energy throughout his twenties and had shaped his physique accordingly. He was six-foot-one, of medium build and had broad, muscular shoulders. Attractive, his short back and sides, with long sideburns was generally concealed by a well-worn, wide-brimmed hat. He was rarely seen out of his dark-blue, heavy denim overalls and buckled leather work boots. There were days when he loathed having to get up at the crack of dawn to commence work, but for the most part he relished the challenges each day brought.

Hosea Jackson, their ranch hand, was no stranger at having to step up before his time either. He was orphaned as a young teenager when his African-American parents became victims of the civil and political unrest of the time. The night after organising and speaking at a local rally demanding more civil and economic rights, the mood was high in the Jackson household. Their house was a hive of activity, with other community leaders and friends coming and going most hours of the day. They were eagerly following the ideals and teachings of Martin Luther King Jnr, who was fast becoming a prominent voice in the Civil Rights Movement across America. Future rallies were planned, and momentum was building quickly, much to the dismay of those opposed. It was a joyous occasion around the dinner table, and the future seemed a little brighter as the flame of community spirit and optimism burned strong.

Hosea's bedroom was at the back of the house and his parent's at the front. Luckily for him, he didn't hear any disturbance during that fateful night when they were murdered in their sleep, their throats slashed and tongues cut out at the hands of suspected white extremists.

Similar crimes were sporadically being disclosed around the country. The method used was very personal. In every reported case, the cause of death was the same. Police suspected the perpetrators didn't want African-American people to have a voice and chose to slash the throat and cut out the tongue as a symbol of disdain. To add further insult to injury, the same message was left at each crime scene, scrawled in the victim's blood. It simply said: Know Thy Place. Some within the African-American community believed the police were directly involved, as a way to keep them under a regime of oppression. Those who indicated they had proof of this often disappeared, never to be seen or heard from again. The white police force said they had no leads, and the case, along with many others, would remain unsolved.

Shortly after discovering his parents' bodies and surrendering them to the state, because he couldn't afford a funeral, Hosea was forced to board up the family home and relocate to find work. Many of his family's possessions were given away. He retained only what he could carry in a large suitcase. He'd knocked on the Hubbard door two winters ago, offering his services as a ranch hand. Many African-Americans toiled underpaid and overworked, and Hosea would be no different.

The thud of muddy work boots on the porch startled Eileen as she brought the hot dinner plates to the table.

'The meal smells wonderful Mrs Hubbard.'

'Thank you Hosea, my husband's favourite, steak with eggs and potato mash. Please, for the last time, call me Eileen.'

'Sorry, Mrs Hubbard, I mean, Eileen, just habit.

'That's alright. Now sit and eat before it gets cold.'

As he ate, Hosea was grateful to have a roof over his head, food in his belly and to be cared for once again, even if his employers were white and couldn't afford to pay him.

Chapter Four

Memories

D r Marcus Strickland paused a moment before he pushed open his office door with his foot, struggling with an overflowing box of stationery, books and a potted plant. The sign on the door made it real: Dr Marcus Strickland – Forensic Pathologist. Day one of his working career would begin the following morning and he wanted it to be a smooth, hassle-free event. As he wrangled with the box, the corner of his new desk impacted his mid-thigh resulting in a stumble, a cursed word or two and loss of connection with the box which slid across the table, finally coming to a stop just shy of the opposite edge.

'Phew. That was close,' he said, as he dusted himself off and hobbled, temporarily lame, towards his new plastic-wrapped office chair.

There was quite a job ahead of him, since the former storage area needed some personal touches to turn it into a functional, thought-provoking space. Reaching into the box, he removed his framed degree certificate and found a place for it on a hook directly behind the desk. He stood back to admire it briefly, reflecting on the doubts and hurdles he'd worked through to complete his studies. The potted plant he placed to the right of his telephone, nearest the window, to maximise the indirect light. The Monstera deliciosa was a graduation present from his parents, to remind him he still needed to care equally for the living. Despite having never owned a plant before, he was hopeful at being able to keep it alive. The books found their way to a bookshelf. Most were medical in nature, but there was also one on caring for indoor plants that he had yet to read. His over-sized coffee cup, given to him by his best mate at university because of the message written on it - If you think you're having a bad day, remember you're still alive - took its place next to the coffee cannister and kettle on the credenza.

For his twenty-five years of age he looked every bit a scientist. He was tall and lanky. His mid-length light brown hair, parted left of centre, was kept in place with a modest amount of Brylcreem. His otherwise plain appearance was made more sophisticated with round, thick-rimmed spectacles and a raspberry-red bow tie. His brown vest with a light-red check pattern, and matching jacket and pants, finished the look.

The next day, shortly after meeting his new secretary, Delores, his phone rang. His career had begun.

* **

William Ellis had barely spoken a word in the past twenty-five years about the circumstances surrounding his sister's death, and he had shielded his children successfully from several reporters who came sniffing around, wanting an exclusive. The mystery of his sister's untimely demise was the talk of the small community. Everything from an unfortunate accident to murder was being touted. One particularly vicious rumour he'd heard was that, after a fight, William had doused his sister in brandy and then set her alight while he stood back laughing. This formed the basis for his foundation of silence on the issue.

After initially being considered by the police as the prime suspect in her horrific passing, he was quickly and reasonably ruled out when witnesses were interviewed, and the timeline of events established. The autopsy was incomplete, inconclusive and highly speculative as to the cause of death, and William himself didn't have a theory that made any sense. The police were convinced it was murder, or, at the very least, stated she was a victim of foul play, contrary to the forensic pathologist's report. However, given the pieces of the forensic puzzle, the lack of witnesses, and with no suspect identified from the cross-referencing of latent fingerprints found at the scene, they were left with an open, unsolved case gathering dust in a filing cabinet.

Fresh-faced, green-eyed Dr Strickland was the first professional on the scene that night, along with a police officer. The crime scene was thoroughly photographed before the remains were removed for further examination, to establish cause of death. William had read the autopsy report numerous times over the years, and three things still puzzled him: the cause, the intensity of the fire and the timeframe. Dr Strickland had explained his hypothesis based on the visible evidence at the scene, and the lack of any witnesses to the actual combustion event.

According to William, Margaret had made her way up the carpeted stairs and across the landing before removing her shoes. Entering her bedroom with her stockings on, the friction between them and the shagpile carpet could have sufficiently built up, charging her body with static electricity. The brandy she'd consumed was possibly ignited by a static spark, perhaps as she brushed or ran her fingers through her hair. The other plausible explanation mentioned in the report was electrocution by arcing from the light bulb connecting to her static charge. This could have rendered her motionless, causing the ignition of the brandy in her throat, then stomach, resulting in her inability to scream.

Still, the intensity of the fire puzzled him, and initially Dr Strickland too. He'd ordered Margaret's medical file, to scrutinise any pre-existing or undiagnosed medical conditions which could have contributed to the otherwise inexplicable. From previous blood work, he discovered that Margaret had high levels of phosphorus in her system. William mentioned, at the time, that his sister had never indicated she had any disease or illness she was being treated for. This may have meant she didn't know her kidneys were unable to filter out the excess phosphate from her body, or that she'd chosen not to reveal her medical issue to loved ones. William also mentioned that, over the last decade or so, she had always drunk brandy nightly, suggesting dependence, which may have brought about the improper kidney function. Dr Strickland further indicated in his report that the intensity of the fire was likely fuelled by the brandy, excess phosphorous and her own body fat.

So why hadn't the fire consumed other flammable items nearby as well? William had asked. Dr Strickland used the example of a candle to explain. The candle is able to burn without being extinguished because the wax surrounding the wick is its fuel source. Naturally, a curtain or piece of paper can catch fire if it passes over the heat source, but it won't necessarily do so if it is next to or under the flame, as heat predominately goes up and not outwards. Margaret's body was able to burn up almost completely until its own fuel sources - the brandy, phosphorous, body fat, clothing and oxygen levels in the room ran too low and it extinguished.

So how was it possible to see almost complete destruction of her body in such a short period of time? For a body to be cremated didn't the temperatures have to be in the vicinity of 1800 degrees Fahrenheit or more? William had enquired, having done some research of his own on the subject. Dr Strickland agreed the timeframe was rather short, because a standard cremation, under all the right conditions, taking into account body mass and bone density, would normally be anywhere between ninety minutes to four hours. Dehydrated bone fragments would still remain. These would then be pulverised, giving the remains a fine, grainy, ash-like consistency. In Margaret's case, much of her skeleton had already turned to ash. She was average height and carrying a little more weight than she may have liked for her thirty-four years of age. The dress she wore that night was made from rayon - her preferred fabric, apparently, as most of her garments were made from it. Rayon is noted as being more flammable than polyester, nylon, wool or silk. Putting all the evidence together, it was possible the fire that engulfed her burned intensely and quickly enough to almost entirely consume her in one to one-and-a-half hours. As side notes, Dr Strickland mentioned in his report that he found no evidence of any accelerant, nor any evidence of suicide or foul play. The bedroom window had been closed and locked from the inside. The bedroom door had also been closed throughout the combustion event, which limited the amount of oxygen available to fuel the fire. Margaret was a non-smoker, and no cigarettes or matches were found in the bedroom.

It had been a quarter of a century, but William's memories of the night remained fresh.

* * *

Dr Strickland had only seen one other seemingly inexplicable case of Spontaneous Human Combustion (SHC) in his five years as a forensic pathologist, and that was as an intern shortly after graduating from his Forensic Science degree. The circumstances and evidence weren't too dissimilar to Margaret Ellis' case. Although the official findings were recorded as death by misadventure, the evidentiary and scientific links were flimsy and drew a closer conclusion to SHC. His report had been rewritten to fit with the acceptable standard of the time and he was reminded that future reports needed to follow suit. Despite initially feeling a sense of injustice, he filed the case and got on with his career, heeding his superiors advice. The notes of his initial observations of the scene, kept in a personal journal, were as clear to him now as the day he'd first written them.

The large blue flame flickered ever so slightly as the cremated remains crumbled beneath it. Gazing upon it as I moved closer, the flame diminished in size and intensity as if it were a cautious animal in retreat. The bluish grey haze in the air hung florally sweet, but no flowers, perfume or incense could be found.

The flame's source material was unrecognisable and unfamiliar at first glance, until I spotted a crooked row of teeth protruding from where the flame emanated. Curiosity and inquisitiveness abruptly gave way to disbelief and horror. Fighting the instant nausea and urge to vomit, I glanced back towards the unfortunate victim and spied the emergence of the flame again. It was very much alive and seemed to be teasing me, I took a step towards it and again its intensity diminished.

Death hovered in the air. Surely there was nothing further the flame could consume. What was it waiting for? How could someone have burned up so completely without greatly affecting the combustible surrounds? It defies physics as I understand it.

Chapter Five

Haemorrhage

Although seven months pregnant, Eileen saw no harm in having a drink every now and then, to calm her nerves as she put it. She was more like her aunt than she knew. During the weekly food shop, she would call into the local liquor store to purchase Arrabidine, a berry liqueur, and Rectified Spirits. She would always say it was for her husband. The attendant, without saying a word, smiled as he dutifully packed the paper bag. He knew her husband, Tomas, to be a non-drinker. She'd been told her Aunty Margaret used to drink brandy, but for some reason Eileen couldn't stomach it. She remembered very little about her mother and aunt, as she was only six when both died. Her father had rarely spoken about their deaths, and she now wondered about the circumstances as she consumed her drink.

* * *

William hadn't seen his eldest daughter in a while and thought it would be a good idea to call in and check on her. He also wanted to offer a hand in making some repairs to her residence before his first grandchild was born. William wasn't an outwardly emotional man and it was often hard to read his thoughts. Inwardly he felt things deeply and had been permanently wounded by the untimely death of his wife and sister all those years prior. Consequently, he never remarried.

Eileen answered the knock at the door and was surprised to see her father standing there.

'Hello sweetheart,' he said, arms outstretched.

'Dad, hi. It's great to see you!' she remarked as she embraced him. 'I'm surprised you didn't call ahead. Tomas would have loved to have seen you, but he's in the top paddock seeding.' Eileen invited him in, closed the door and then slowly waddled into the kitchen to put the kettle on.

'Oh well. Never mind. I wanted to see how you were and offer my handyman services to do some repair work for you. I know you have a list as long as your arm, and with Tomas working so hard to keep the ranch up and running, I wanted this to be a gift to you before the baby arrives,' William said, a lump developing in his throat.

'Aww, Dad, that's such a wonderful thought, and Tomas won't mind a bit. Let's have a cuppa, and we can discuss the most pressing needs. I also have something I wish to ask of you,' she said as she brought the tray of food and drink to the dining table where they both sat down.

'The most pressing need really is the front steps. They're full of rot, and I doubt the hand-rail will support my weight for much longer.' Eileen offered her father his usual cup of unadulterated black coffee and a shortbread biscuit.

'Okay, sweetheart. Consider them replaced. I've brought some hickory wood and tools with me. You have me for the rest of the afternoon and all day tomorrow.'

'Thanks, Dad. It will be such a weight off my mind not to be afraid to enter or exit the house on my own in my present condition. The next job would be to mend a dozen or so wooden shingles on the roof as they've worked their way loose and leak when it rains,' Eileen went on. 'Also, some insulation around the windows would greatly help with heating the place. Perhaps later tonight, when Tomas returns, you can both put your heads together to reconstruct my old baby cot in the spare room?' Eileen smiled and offered another shortbread biscuit.

'Very well,' William remarked. 'You've always been good at bribery!' They both laughed. 'You said you had something you wished to ask of me?'

'Yes, I did. I've been thinking a lot about Mum lately. I guess it relates to changing hormones and maternal instinct,' Eileen said, as she rested her hands on her stomach.

William sat silently, staring at his coffee as his daughter spoke. He knew the day would come, when his children wanted answers. The question was whether he was ready to give them.

'I only have a few memories of her and I know you haven't said much over the years because you wanted to protect us. I guess I just –.'

'It's okay. I wondered when you might ask, and it's a discussion I've been meaning to have with you and your siblings for some time now. It's been easier to put it off.' He looked up from his coffee, tears welling.

'Oh, Dad. I didn't mean to upset you,' Eileen said, now feeling awful.

'You haven't, sweetheart. It's high time I got this off my chest. I've bottled it up for far too long. I'm afraid if I continue to do so it'll give me a hernia. Your mother meant the world to me; she was my rock. She kept me focussed and in line. If it wasn't for the fact I had three children under the age of six to care for, I think I would've completely unravelled. The emotional rollercoaster of feeling elated that I had a son at the same time as I was grieving the loss of my wife was incredibly overwhelming.'

William paused a moment as he reflected on the night he'd lost Bernadette. He got up from his chair and made his way to the window before continuing.

'I had Henry in my arms as the room cleared of medical personnel. I recall Bernadette smiling at me as I cried tears of joy at being blessed with a son. The labour had been un-eventful but long, and she said she was very tired. I kissed her on the forehead. She smiled again and then drifted off to sleep. She looked so peaceful, lying there after the delivery. I knew she must have been exhausted, so I let her be. About half an hour later, when the midwife came in to check on Bernadette, she couldn't wake her. The emergency alarm on the wall was so loud it shattered the bliss and Henry started to cry. We were thrust into a scene of utter pandemonium as nurses and doctors descended on us from all directions and attempted to resuscitate her. The autopsy concluded that she had died peacefully from an internal postpartum haemorrhage. As a result, I struggled to bond with Henry. Every time I held him or looked at him, I was reminded that Bernadette had died.

I didn't want to feel that way. I had a beautiful son to care for who would carry on the family name, but I struggled to process the circumstances of her loss. When she died, I felt robbed and angry. I didn't have a chance to say goodbye or tell her I loved her one more time.'

He paused again to take out a handkerchief and blow his nose.

'Your grandparents and Aunty Margaret helped a lot in raising you all, and looking back on it now, without their assistance, you would have had a very different upbringing.'

'Oh, Dad. I had no idea it was that traumatic. I recall us all going to the hospital as a family, but instead of Mum coming home with us, Aunty Margie did.'

'Yes, that's right. I called to tell her what had happened, and she immediately offered to help. Shortly thereafter she moved in with us.'

'Speaking of Aunty Margie, I know she died in a fire, upstairs in her bedroom at our old house when I was about six. Do you know how it happened?' Eileen said as she left the table to get more shortbread from the kitchen.

There was a long pause while William relived the events that had caused him to discover his late sister's body. The hair on his forearms and on the back of his neck slowly rose. He waited until Eileen had made her way back from the kitchen and sat down before he answered her question.

'I still have the forensic pathologists report on her death, but the cause wasn't exactly determined. I've probably read it a dozen or so times over the years, each time hoping the words on the page will change and make sense to me, but they don't. There were too many assumptions and not enough facts. I guess that's what annoys me the most. I'm sorry. It's probably not what you wanted to hear - that her death was essentially unexplained - but that is all I know,' William said, partly relieved to have finally broken the ice on the subject.

'It's okay. I understand. I was mostly curious is all. Whilst we're talking about Mum and Aunty Margie, there's something else I remembered recently that I don't think I ever told you about,' Eileen said, pouring her father another coffee.

'Oh, and what would that be?' William was apprehensive. He reached for his fourth, and not necessarily last, shortbread biscuit of the afternoon. Eileen smirked.

'Remember when I was sixteen, and went to hospital after I fell off Saintly Sapphire?'

'How could I forget? I thought we'd lost you. You were unconscious, and your left knee had been trodden into the mud. I didn't leave your hospital bedside from the time you were admitted until you woke three days later. I remember pacing the corridor for what seemed like hours, praying you would be alright. I'm still convinced I wore out the linoleum, right down to the concrete beneath. After you came out of surgery, the doctors told me you had swelling on the brain, and whilst they were able to repair most of the damage to your left knee, your leg would be in a calliper for at least six months to aid healing. Your grandparents had to take care of Geraldine and Henry and the ranch, as I refused to do anything but stay with you. I felt guilty and responsible for what had happened. I didn't know at the time the horse was lame. It broke my heart to have to call the veterinarian and have him put to sleep. We'd only had him a few short weeks. Old Mr Cassidy felt so guilty he hadn't noticed the symptoms when I told him. His failing eyesight and being preoccupied with the sale of his property caused his ignorance. Some sixteenth birthday present that turned out to be.'

'That's right! That damn calliper. I think it was only three months in the end, because I healed faster than expected. I remember being teased a lot at school for having to wear it and was relieved when it came off. Anyway, I'm getting side-tracked. Whilst I was in the coma, I had a dream, or at least I think it was a dream. I woke in the middle of the night and saw Mum and Aunty Margie standing at the foot of my bed. Initially, I thought they were a couple of nurses, but as I focussed, a familiarity about them dawned on me. They told me how much they loved me, that it wasn't my time, and whilst they'd never intended to leave us, they were watching over us all from afar.'

'I asked Aunty Margie what happened the night of the fire. She bowed her head and Mum took a-hold of her hand. After a short while she stated there were forces at work beyond our control or comprehension, both good and evil. She told me that while she sat drinking brandy at her dresser, she saw a dark but translucent image of a woman, with long black hair appear in the mirror behind her, and then she couldn't move. She began to feel hot and her skin tingled all over, followed by an intoxicating bright white light, and that was all she could recall. She reassured me she was fine and not to worry, as she would continue to watch over and protect us. I remember she gave me a kiss on my forehead, followed by Mum, and then, as they held hands, they vanished.'

'So, there was someone, or something, with Margaret in her bedroom that night? I can scarcely believe it. The police and pathologist found no evidence of a third party being involved. That's the first time you've ever told me that, sweetheart,' William said, his tears returning. He reached for his handkerchief. 'It's nice to have your mum and Margaret the centre of conversation again. It's been too long.' William blew his nose.

'Yes. Sorry I didn't tell you sooner. I had forgotten all about it over the years.' Eileen heaved herself out of the chair and gathered the afternoon tea dishes.

'Leave all that. I'll do it. You just sit yourself down,' William said with a smile, as he picked up the afternoon tea tray, put his hand on her shoulder and then made his way to the kitchen.

Waiting for the hot water to fill the sink, William recalled a story of his own, one that his grandfather had told him as a boy. The events had occurred at a relative's ranch several hundred years ago. Mary-Susanna Ellis had been returning from church with her teenage son, Harrelson, in the family's horse and cart. The cart contained two bales of hay, a small barrel of rum and some farming equipment. As they turned into the road leading to the homestead, one of the wheels made a sound like it had worked its way loose. Mary-Susanna stopped the cart, and Harrelson jumped out to inspect it.

A short distance away, on the opposite side of the cart, Harrelson noticed flames coming out the ground, but instead of saying anything, he continued to work on the wheel. His mother had not seen them, her attention focussed on her son. Without any further warning, the ground between the horse and cart split open and the flames raced towards them, increasing in height. There was no time to warn his mother. As the hay in the cart exploded into flame, the horse's tail started to burn, and it panicked and bolted. All Mary-Susanna could do was hold on for her life.

The cart hadn't travelled very far before it flipped, as the wheel Harrelson had been working on, shattered. Harrelson, who'd run after the cart, saw his mother kneeling, motionless. He cautiously approached and to his horror discovered she'd been impaled through the chest by a pitchfork and was surrounded by flame. The horse, the contents of the cart and Mary-Susanna were consumed. Harrelson survived to recount the story having only sustained superficial burns to one of his hands as he tried to assist.

When the local parish sheriff investigated, the only part of Harrelson's tale that couldn't be verified was the fiery crack in the ground, as it had mysteriously closed over. Even the scorching that should have been present, indicating a fire had occurred, was absent. The only evidence was a line of wilted and partially dried grass that intersected the road.

As a boy, William hadn't believed the tale because his grandfather was a known storyteller, and it was too far-fetched to have been real. But now, after Eileen's vision or dream explaining the demise of Margaret under equally horrific circumstances, perhaps he ought to reconsider.

* * *

Tomas and Hosea had been working solidly for about twelve hours when they decided to call it a day. Tomas had taught Hosea how to drive the tractor, and he'd loved every minute of it. Seeding proved to be a weary time of year. The changeable weather often meant long hours when it was favourable to seed, because days could go by when it wasn't. Hosea finished his final turn for the night, cut the engine and grabbed his things. He didn't realise he hadn't put the vehicle fully in the park position, and it had begun to roll silently forward towards Tomas, who had his back turned. Hosea saw movement in the corner of his eye and, turning his head, yelled 'Look out!'

Tomas spun and dived out of the way just in time as the front wheels narrowly missed his right foot. Hosea, by this time, was already in pursuit of the runaway tractor, striding and lunging, eventually managing to jump aboard and bring it to a stop before it went through the neighbour's boundary fence. Sheepishly returning to where Tomas sat on the ground, Hosea launched into a semi-rehearsed, apologetic speech, drawing to his employer's attention his severe lack of preparedness.

'I'm so sorry, Tomas. I don't know what could have happened. I was certain I did everything you taught me. I clearly didn't put the handbrake on. I really enjoy driving the tractor, but if you don't want me to do it anymore, I completely understand.'

Tomas let him finish. Then extended his hand and Hosea pulled him up. Putting his hands on Hosea's shaking shoulders, Tomas look him straight in the eyes and said, 'I'm okay. No harm done. It's been a lesson learned. We've worked a long day, and in future both of us need to remember to be more careful and call it quits before we're overtaken by exhaustion.'

The short trip home in the truck was a sombre one, with neither uttering a word. Hosea, racked with guilt that he nearly killed his friend and employer, stared out the passenger-side window, secretively wiping tears from his eyes. Meanwhile, Tomas was pondering just how close he'd come to leaving his wife and unborn child husband-and fatherless.

Chapter Six

Shock

Caroline Malloney was only seven when her father, a former labourer in the construction industry, was retrenched from his job. The government was forced to cease all new road, rail, bridge and tunnel developments and pulled funding from many other projects. The minimal severance pay he received for his years of service quickly dried up as household expenses chewed into it, and the purchase and consumption of hard liquor began to take its toll. Night after night, Caroline just wanted to make the noise outside her bedroom door stop - the yelling, the arguments, the crashing of dishes and glass. During those times she'd cover her ears or wrap a pillow around her head. Her teddy bear became her comfort and security blanket. She relied upon him. She took teddy everywhere, even to school.

During the early 1930s, making ends meet was tough for most middle-and working-class families. If you lost your job under any circumstance, you'd be hard pressed to find another. Even if you were self-employed, customers you'd once relied upon had no money to spend on the goods you had to sell. Keeping food on the table became the number one priority for many, but not all. In the Malloney household, meals went from two per day to one every second day.

Through sudden, unfortunate luck, the death of her

grandfather, a widower, left a freehold house and land, some savings and a room full of books to Caroline's mother in 1929. The family moved into the residence in Louisville shortly before The Great Depression hit, which fortunately kept a roof over their heads since they didn't have a mortgage to pay. Occasionally friends of the family would stay for a week or two whilst planning their next move after the bank foreclosed on their homes and evicted them.

Caroline loved to read, and a room full of books almost replaced the need for teddy. Often, she would read aloud to teddy, as he was the only one who would listen. Whilst the economic world and the fabric of society around her collapsed, and the adults in it did their best to deal with the fallout, Caroline immersed herself in school and books. She gave anything to escape the negativity surrounding her at home.

Attending school was an escape from one drama into the hardship of another. Children from several grades were grouped together because resources were scarce. Only those teachers with a true love for teaching remained in the profession, and even then, many taught without taking home a regular pay cheque to support their own families. Sharing books between students, huddled together in winter just to stay warm as the cold and snow built up outside, was normal. Similarly, in summer, school would sometimes be cancelled as the heat and dust was too hazardous.

As the years went by, the number of books in the house diminished as both Caroline and her mother bartered them for food, items of clothing or other necessities. Caroline would sit for hours and hours sorting and flicking through most of them. The ones she didn't understand or that didn't interest her she placed in one corner of the room for bartering. The few she had selected to retain she placed in a wooden crate and tucked it away under her bed for safe keeping.

One day, at the beginning of her teenage years, Caroline returned home from school to find her father passed out, flat on his back on the living room floor. She no longer raised an eyebrow or rolled him onto his side as her mother had instructed. It was practically a daily occurrence and she was done caring. She struggled to understand why her mother hadn't adopted the same mindset, particularly as she was the main target of his abuse. After discovering her mother wasn't home, she made her way to her room, immersed herself in the latest *Dick and Jane* book a friend had given her and didn't come out until morning.

Her mother's scream woke her early the next day. Upon hearing it, she sat bolt upright in bed, causing several books to fall to the floor. Her scream had a different intonation to it from the one Caroline heard when her father used his fists to resolve a dispute he'd often start, so she rushed to her mother's aid.

It was the first time she had seen a dead body. His face and neck were covered in chunks of watery vomit. Her mother was on her knees beside him, weeping as she nervously stroked his hair. For all the pain, anguish and beatings she'd endured over the years, she apparently still loved him. Caroline hadn't been close to him for as long as she could remember, and it came as a relief to her that he was gone, rather than feeling any sadness about his passing.

*   *   *

Caroline's mother must have sensed economic doom on the horizon when she was gifted the savings from her father back in 1929. Instead of depositing the funds in a bank, she kept most of the money hidden in several large glass jars under the wood pile in the back yard. Due to her husband's incapacitated state most of the time, the task of cutting firewood fell to her, so she knew her hiding place would remain a secret. Her intention all along was to use those funds for Caroline's education, and because she had done so well in school, the opportunity to attend university presented itself. Many teachers who'd had the privilege of imparting their knowledge to Caroline in the classroom often commented to her mother that she was mature beyond her years and fiercely independent. Her mother never let on about the issues they faced in private and always came across as agreeable and appreciative. Through deliberate intent, Caroline chose to be invisible when it came to her father. She'd only found herself on the wrong side of his fists twice - once when coming to her mother's aid after the first time he punched and pushed her to the floor, and the other when she accidentally smashed a bottle of whisky whilst errantly swinging teddy in the kitchen. She swore to herself there wouldn't be a third occurrence, and there never was.

Dr Caroline Malloney was a ground-breaking physician in the field of teratology (congenital abnormalities) and her research papers and case studies were the talk of many a medical conference. She wasn't short of case studies either, as the turbulent civil and political times were causing more to turn to drink, rivalling the rate of consumption during The Great Depression. In the medical world, almost completely dominated by men, she had to fight for every word to be taken seriously and had developed a thick skin over the years. She was as proud of her work as she was about her appearance. From tip to toe, every aspect of her outfit had a place. Her naturally straight, dark brown, mid-length hair sat perfectly across her broad, voluptuous frame, kept off her symmetrical face with a simple black headband. Her choice of work attire was a black two-piece pant suit - conservative but on trend. Her favourite pair of shoes were three-inch Pony Hair stilettos. Because her work was so demanding and mentally tough, she kept herself fit with yoga and regularly walked to and from work.

At Eileen's last check-up, her obstetrician had referred her to Dr Malloney after observing an abnormality during the ultrasound. It wasn't unusual for medical professionals to consult one another in this regard, and this was explained to Eileen to allay any fears. Tomas had driven Eileen to the clinic for her check-up and used the time in town to grab a couple of second-hand parts for the tractor, so seeding could continue. As Eileen entered the clinic and made her way to the reception desk, a bright and bubbly young receptionist greeted her.

'Hello. How can I help you?'

'Hello. I'm Eileen Hubbard. I have an appointment with Dr Malloney at eleven.'

The receptionist flicked through the large appointment book on her desk. After a moment she said, 'Ah yes. Please take a seat, Mrs Hubbard. Dr Malloney is running a little behind today but shouldn't be long.'

Eileen managed a genuine smile and then made her way to a dark red sofa across the room, which was already partially occupied by another expectant mother looking more than a little distressed.

'Are you okay?' Eileen gently enquired of the woman who was breathing heavily and sweating profusely.

'Uh, hum, fine thanks,' she said semi-breathlessly, beads of sweat dripping from her furrowed brow. She was twisting the life out of a hand towel in her lap as if it were the neck of a chicken.

'Okay,' Eileen said under her breath as she rolled her eyes and picked up a magazine from the side table to read.

Fifteen minutes elapsed before Eileen looked across again at the woman with whom she shared the sofa, to see the remains of the unfortunate hand towel in several pieces next to her and on the floor. The woman was now sitting on her hands to stop the fidgeting, whilst gently rocking backwards and forwards, muttering to herself. Dr Malloney's work dealt with many expectant mothers who were also addicts. Eileen was observing withdrawal symptoms, only she didn't know it.

'Mrs Eileen Hubbard, please,' the nurse said as she opened the door to the waiting room.

'That would be me,' Eileen said as she placed the magazine back on the side table and struggled, momentarily, to break free from the comfortable sofa. The nurse smiled as she indicated the way through to Dr Malloney's office.

'Good morning, Eileen. I'm Dr Malloney. Please come in.'

They shook hands and Eileen took her seat as the nurse closed the consulting room door behind her and drew a small curtain on the door's glass panel for privacy.

'Do you know why you're here to see me today, Eileen?' Dr Malloney said.

'No, not really. My obstetrician told me you wanted to see me based on my last ultrasound. Is something wrong?' Eileen thought about the magazine she'd been reading in the waiting room fifteen minutes earlier, about caring for disabled children with genetic abnormalities.

'Do you know what my speciality is?' Dr Malloney asked.

'Genetic abnormalities,' Eileen said with certainty.

'Err, yes, that's correct Eileen.' Dr Malloney was surprised by the accuracy of her answer. 'Let me get right to the point.' Dr Malloney left her chair, made her way to the corner of her desk in front of Eileen and sat there. 'Your ultrasound revealed a healthy baby. However, on each hand and foot there are six digits instead of five.'

A very pregnant pause lingered in the air. Eileen was

stunned. With tears welling in her eyes, she instinctively looked at her own hands as she attempted to take in what she had just been told.

'How much do you drink, Eileen?'

'Huh? What?' Eileen said in a daze, still studying her own hands.

Dr Malloney repeated her question. 'How much do you drink each day?'

'Umm I don't –.'

'The abnormality seen on your ultrasound is consistent with alcohol abuse, and I'm fairly certain you were drinking before and during your pregnancy for this to occur,' Dr Malloney said, insistently.

'No, no, no!' Eileen shook her head in disbelief, and eventually buried her head in her hands, bursting into tears.

As the daughter of an alcoholic father, Dr Malloney had heard all the excuses condoning addictive behaviour over the years. It had left a permanent imprint on her brain like a tattoo. Each patient she saw came with their own unique set of denials, excuses and lies. She chose the field of teratology because it was an area of medicine not widely understood or researched, and she wanted to help mothers appreciate the consequences of destructive behaviour, whether it had been learned from a parent or adopted through circumstance. She was determined to restrict the same addictive behavioural patterns she'd observed growing up by taking a tough-love and direct approach with her patients. Over the years the gloss had worn off her chosen career path, and whilst compassion and empathy had their place, neither came naturally to her.

After a moment Dr Malloney took the seat next to Eileen's, grabbed her hand and, looking directly into her teary, bloodshot eyes, quietly but sternly said, 'I know this may have come as quite a shock, but you need to quit the alcohol immediately, Eileen, for the sake of your baby. You have eight weeks to go. I'm going to prescribe you some medication to combat withdrawal symptoms, as well as Thiamine and Folic Acid for the baby's developing health. I want you to take 10mg of Diazepam four times a day for five days. Take 1.4mg of Thiamine orally daily and 400 micrograms of Folic Acid daily. I'll write it all down for you and, Eileen, no alcohol at all. If you feel you need a drink, consume a large glass of water and call me. Okay?'

Chapter Seven

Lies

Eileen left Dr Malloney's office visibly devastated by the news she had received. Her head hung low, her shoulders were rigid and her face was red and strained. She could see herself ending up like the woman she'd shared the waiting room sofa with, if she didn't heed the doctor's advice. There was precious little time to think. The one thing she knew for certain was that Tomas must never find out. He was a gentle, hardworking soul, but Eileen was afraid how he might react if he discovered her drinking (the extent of which she had also kept from him) had caused the abnormality. An act of God was one thing, but a conscious decision to drink nightly before and during pregnancy was quite another, even if she hadn't been fully aware of the risks involved.

She took several deep breaths as she waited on the street corner until Tomas pulled up in the truck and helped her in. A nervous energy filled her as she prepared for the question she knew was coming.

'How was the appointment, love? Is everything on track?' Tomas asked, right on cue.

'Everything's fine, progressing well. Dr Malloney has requested I increase my vitamin intake, so we'll need to make a stop at the drug store to get this prescription filled before we return home.' She hated having to lie to her husband, but she thought she was choosing the lesser of two evils.

'Sure, honey. That's easy.' Tomas beamed from ear to ear.

Phew. Disaster averted, she thought, but guilt gnawed at her stomach in light of her husband's excitement. *If only I hadn't used the bottle to deal with my insecurities and anxiety all those years ago, I wouldn't be addicted now.* Admitting this to herself was a difficult first step. As Eileen gazed out the window, staring aimlessly into the street, she spied acquaintances and total strangers passing by. She anguished over how perfect their little lives appeared to be and wondered why hers couldn't be more so.

They pulled up at the drug store, Eileen asked Tomas to head to the corner store to grab some groceries on the ranch account, handing him a list, because supplies were low at home. It was also a ruse to ensure he would be elsewhere while she continued to perpetuate the lie.

Waiting in line at the prescription counter she said to herself, *God I could really go a dri–*. Stopping mid-sentence, she realised how ingrained in the process she was, and that the next eight weeks were likely to be hell. Eileen could see movement out the corner of her eye as a woman made a beeline for her position in the queue. It was an old school friend, Susan Staffordshire.

'Eileen? Eileen Ellis? Is that really you?' Susan bellowed as she forced her way through the queue to position herself alongside her.

'Susan. Hell, it's been years, and its Hubbard now.' Eileen tried to sound polite.

'Susan Staffordshire-Routledge myself these days, and, oh, is this your first?' Susan's question was so loud it drew everyone's attention to Eileen's figure. She'd never had an inside voice.

'Yes, it is. Only eight weeks to go now,' Eileen replied, hoping the floor would open up and swallow her.

'Well, congratulations. I have two myself. They're with the nanny, so I can have some retail therapy time.' Susan bragged, laughing. 'Well, gotta run. My money won't spend itself. Nice seeing you.'

'You too. Bye.' Eileen waved half-heartedly, but Susan had already scurried out the front door.

Eileen hadn't thought highly of Susan back in high school. They mixed in different circles and had rarely crossed paths. Susan was the classic over achiever whilst Eileen liked to fly under the radar. After all these years, her opinion of Susan hadn't changed. The woman had an indirect way of sucking the life out of a conversation, and oxygen out of a room by always putting herself on a pedestal. Her father had made his fortune in mineral mining, and she loved spending Daddy's money. Eileen was secretively envious of her social position, but would never admit it.

Returning home, the brand-new front steps looked like a welcoming, shiny beacon on an otherwise-gloomy day. Thanks to her father's handyman skills, this was one less worry Eileen would have for her safety as she came and went from the house.

While Tomas unloaded the truck, Eileen waddled inside

with purpose and frantically searched the pantry for the Arrabidine and Rectified Spirits. Once located, she made her way to the sink with them. As she popped the cork on the Arrabidine bottle, the aroma instantly tickled her nostrils and teased her tastebuds. She made the mistake of taking a deep breath. The invitation was simply too irresistible and the bottle found its way to her lips. She expected a pang of guilt to subdue her, but surprisingly there was none. As she went to take another mouthful she heard the front door open and immediately upended the bottle to drain into the sink. The pang of guilt that kicked in at that moment was purely financial. *What a waste.* She threw a used dishtowel over the Rectified Spirits bottle just as Tomas entered the kitchen with a large paper bag of groceries under each arm. Pouring herself a glass of water, she popped open her recently acquired vitamin pills and began her new routine as prescribed.

Chapter Eight

Delivery

As Eileen's due date inched closer, she requested Tomas stay nearer to the house to be within earshot of her call should she need him at a moment's notice. That moment came sooner than expected for both of them.

Eileen had just finished taking a warm shower and had wrapped her wet hair in a towel. She wiped the bathroom mirror clear of condensation, and as she began to apply her moisturiser, her waters broke. She was six weeks out from her due date and panic set in. Tomas was on the roof mending some guttering when he heard her cry out.

'Tomas, we need to get to the hospital immediately! My water's broken. Hurry!' Eileen's tone was full of desperation.

Tomas, startled by the announcement, slipped as he descended the ladder, dropping his hammer onto a pile of sheet metal below. Cursing at the noise it made, he opened the back door to find his wife on the bathroom floor, naked, shivering and in a state of shock. He managed to get her to her feet and then to the edge of the bath, where she took a seat and gratefully accepted the towel he handed her.

Meanwhile, Tomas headed to the bedroom to collect a night gown and overcoat. He then called the hospital, advising them of their impending arrival, before he helped Eileen to the truck for the ten-minute journey.

'Don't push, honey. Focus on your breathing. Deep breaths in and out, in and out,' Tomas said, strapping her into the passenger seat, all the while breathing with her.

'I'm not pushing, god damn it!' Eileen snapped, between deep breaths.

A look of shock crossed Tomas' face. It had been some time since he'd heard his wife curse like that.

'We haven't packed a bloody overnight bag either, Tomas. Oh, I hate being disorganised,' Eileen groaned breathlessly.

'It's okay, honey. I'll just grab the toiletries bag and a change of clothes for you. Anything else we'll get later.' Tomas remained remarkably calm.

Arriving at the front entrance of the Louisville County Hospital, Eileen was assisted by a security guard and the midwife, Celia Di Santo, into a wheelchair, while Tomas found a car park. Celia was a robust, middle-aged woman whose face and demeanour didn't reflect her years. She was only five-foot and had an Italian accent. She came across as young and vibrant and clearly had a love for her job.

'Hello Eileen. I'm Celia Di Santo, your midwife for delivery today. I understand you're about six weeks out from your due date?' Celia took charge of the wheelchair and entered the hospital, picking up the pace.

'Yes, that's right. Oh God it's too ... early.' Eileen said, between puffs and pants.

'It's okay, Eileen. You're in the best place. We're going to take very good care of you and your baby.' Celia rounded a corner into a delivery room, where another nurse was ready to assist.

'I'm just going to scrub up, and Nurse Sullivan here will assist you out of the wheelchair. Okay?'

'Okay.' Eileen winced, gripping the wheelchair to resist another contraction.

Tomas raced in through the hospital entrance and headed immediately to the reception counter, to enquire after his wife. The receptionist told him which direction to head and indicated there was a public waiting room just outside the delivery room. He was full of nervous energy - a mix of excitement and anxiety. Reaching the waiting room in record time, he took a seat for what seemed like less than a second before he began pacing. He would soon be a first-time father and it was all happening faster than either of them had anticipated.

As Eileen's contractions increased in frequency and strength, Nurse Sullivan recommended she no longer walk around but lie down to help conserve her energy, in case it was required for a lengthy labour process. After opting for nitrous oxide over an epidural, because she was afraid of needles, Eileen felt relaxed, almost delirious, and experienced little pain. While Celia monitored the baby's heart rate and waited for established labour to progress to full dilation, Nurse Sullivan took a moment to pull her aside, to inform her of Eileen's recent medical history, as provided in part by Dr Malloney. The alcohol addiction, medication and abnormalities gave her the full picture at a glance. A shared moment of eye contact between the pair communicated the fact that the remainder of the delivery could be troublesome.

When Eileen's labour reached the twelve-hour mark, exhaustion had well and truly set in.

'It's okay, Eileen. I want you to stop pushing for the moment. Have a rest and I'll let you know when to try again.'

'God damn it. I don't know how much more of this I can take,' Eileen said, completely exasperated.

Celia checked on the baby's heart rate, which was slightly elevated but not above the normal expected range during a natural delivery.

'You're doing just fine, Eileen. The first time can often be the longest as your body has never done this before. Just keep pushing when I tell you to and it will all be over soon.' Celia's words of reassurance offered Eileen little comfort in her state of delirium.

Three hours later, Eileen successfully delivered an underweight five-pound-nine-ounce baby girl. She was totally spent, and upon being told she'd given birth to a daughter, she could only manage a few short moments holding her before the remaining strength in her arms failed causing her to surrender her precious child to the midwife. The baby was then whisked away to the nursery in a humidicrib.

Tomas was dozing in the waiting room, when Nurse Sullivan gently woke him.

'Mr Hubbard?' There was no immediate response, so she tried again. 'Mr Hubbard, I have some good news for you.

Your wife has just delivered a baby girl. Both she and the baby are fine. Congratulations.'

'Oh my God. I'm a father? When can I see them?' Tomas sprang out of his chair and moved toward the door.

'Your wife is asleep. The fifteen-hour labour took its toll, so it's best we let her rest for now. I will check with the nursery staff and let you know when they are ready for you to see your daughter. While you're waiting, if you're hungry or want a coffee, there's a cafeteria just down the corridor to your right. I'll come and find you when I know more,' Nurse Sullivan said, knowing a difficult conversation might soon follow if he was unaware of his daughter's abnormalities.

Tomas, unable to contain his excitement, burst through the cafeteria's double doors and announced at the top of his voice that he was a father for the first time. A couple of sets of eyes turned. Another couple in the far corner clapped, and someone said congratulations. Having ordered a sandwich and coffee, he almost gave himself indigestion as he hoovered them down out of sheer excitement. He was about to order a second coffee when Nurse Sullivan entered and motioned for him to follow her. It would be a few minutes before they reached the nursery, and she thought it best to appraise Tomas of his daughter's extra digits before he saw her.

'Before we proceed, I just want to let you know a few things about your daughter.'

Tomas glanced across at Nurse Sullivan with a slightly puzzled look.

'She was born with extra digits on both hands and feet. Being a premature baby, she is also a little underweight. She will have –.'

'Digits?'

'Yes, an extra finger and toe on each hand and foot. She will have some tubes in her nose and throat to help her breath as her lungs weren't fully formed. She will need to stay in hospital for a couple of weeks until she is strong enough to go home.'

'Umm, I'm sorry, but what would cause a baby to be born with extra digits?' Tomas was still trying to get his head around what he was being told.

Being careful not to breach any confidentialities between patient and doctor, Nurse Sullivan responded in general terms.

'There can be many reasons, such as environmental considerations, genetic factors, alcohol or medication abuse, to name a few. Dr Malloney has been called in to further explain that to you.'

Rounding a corner at the end of a long corridor, they arrived at the nursery.

'Here we are. Unfortunately, you can't go in at this time. Premature babies need a pristine environment to limit their chances of lung infection. I shall have a nurse bring your baby's humidicrib over to the viewing window, so you can see her. Congratulations again, Mr Hubbard.' Nurse Sullivan shook his hand and then left.

Tomas' feelings of excitement and nervous energy

had changed in the short walk from the cafeteria. They now included angst and concern, fearful of how his wife would take the news when she woke. A moment passed before his daughter appeared in front of him, and tears welled as he placed his hand on the glass. She was more beautiful than he had envisioned. Fine black hair covered her head. She was so small and yet so precious. Her beautiful long eyelashes shaded her flickering eyes as she lingered between being awake and the land of Z's. Her left hand was clutching at the air, as if in search of a parental finger to latch onto. While Tomas was engrossed in the wonder of new life, Dr Malloney entered the corridor.

'Hello Mr Hubbard, I'm Dr Caroline Malloney. Your daughter's absolutely beautiful, isn't she?' Dr Malloney extended her hand, drawing alongside him.

'She sure is. My little angel.' Tomas shook her hand and placed his other back on the glass, aching to get in there and hold her.

'I have an office just across the hall. Would you join me for a moment?' Dr Malloney indicated the direction.

'Please take a seat. I won't keep you long. I know you've been here for some time and must be exhausted and in need of some decent sleep. I understand Nurse Sullivan told you a little about your daughter's abnormalities?'

'Yes, she did. What would cause something like that?' Tomas asked, with eyes full of concern.

'I saw your wife a few weeks ago. She was referred by her obstetrician, who wanted a second opinion on Eileen's latest ultrasound. With regards to alcohol-induced abnormalities, foetal alcohol syndrome can lead to the development of poly-dactyly - the physical condition of having extra fingers and/or toes. There are seven categories of congenital abnormalities and polydactyly belongs to the category of duplication. Did you know about your wife's drinking, Mr Hubbard?'

'Umm, well, yes. I know she has a glass every now and then, to calm her nerves as she put it, but –.'

'I'm sorry to say it has been quite a bit more than a glass every now and then. This kind of abnormality develops from alcohol abuse, drinking every day for a sustained period, including during pregnancy.'

'Did my wife know about this?'

'Yes. I informed her several weeks ago –.'

'So, you're saying my wife knew about our baby's abnor-malities and kept it from me? As well as hiding how much she drank?'

Tomas sat bolt upright and leant forward to assert some authority. Adrenaline coursed through his veins as his pupils dilated. His fidgety palms became sweaty and his legs restless.

'Let me explain. When we met, I gave her medication to help with alcohol withdrawal symptoms, as well as some vitamins. I believe she has been taking them as she filled a second prescription just two days ago. With alcohol abuse and news of an abnormality during pregnancy, the mother can feel ashamed, embarrassed and ultimately guilty. Upon hearing the information, she must have had a very hard time processing it, and probably felt sparing you the news was easier for her to cope.' Dr Malloney paused, thinking Tomas might respond, but when he kept his head down, she continued.

'I don't want to make any excuses for her behaviour, but I do wish to emphasize that it isn't easy to reduce dependence on alcohol. Apart from being very sore and tired for the next week or so, as a result of the birth, she will also be mentally fragile. With your permission, I would like to arrange for a nurse to visit her daily for the first week or two she's at home, to check on her welfare and make sure she's taking the medication and vitamins I've prescribed. It's vital she be strong enough, and in her right mind, before your baby comes home. That way, you will both cope better with the new arrival, and it makes the transition easier.'

'I understand, Dr Malloney, and that's fine. I'm sorry for getting worked up. I feel so guilty for not realising the extent of her drinking, or why she felt she had to. What did I do wrong?' Tomas said, dejectedly.

'I want to assure you, Mr Hubbard, you haven't done anything wrong. Your wife would have used any time she had alone to indulge and would have measured the amount she drank so it didn't appear as though she was drunk. A little bit often enough would have kept the craving for it in check and would have gone unnoticed. She may have had a predisposition to drinking. Perhaps her mother drank during her pregnancy, resulting in her own compulsion? There can be many reasons, and it will be different for everyone. If you or Eileen have any more questions, please contact me. Here are my details. Now, go back out there and spend some more time with your beautiful daughter.'

Chapter Nine

Diazepam

Eileen spent a week in hospital, healing after the birth, and another week recuperating, as per doctor's orders, on minimal duties at home before her daughter, Josephine Henrietta Hubbard, was allowed to leave the hospital. Dr Malloney ensured the medication she had prescribed for Eileen was being taken via a daily nurse visit, and Tomas used the time to finish rearranging and decorating the nursery in their spare bedroom, with William's help. The two men were close. William treated Tomas as if he was his own son. With common farming interests, and the fact both adored Eileen, there was always something to talk about. Hosea took on more responsibility around the ranch, having proven himself to be reliable, thorough and accurate with the tasks he was given, though he had to step up a little sooner than planned due to the unexpected early arrival of the new Hubbard baby.

The day before Eileen returned home, Tomas visited the hospital to help her pack and to update her on the progress he'd made with the nursery. Tomas also wanted Dr Malloney to visit them both, to outline when their daughter's extra digits could be operated on and removed. They had discussed between themselves, at great length, whether to do anything at all. Simple necessities like gloves and shoes would have to be specially made, and they felt it would be easier, and cheaper in the long run, to be able to buy what was needed just like everyone else. Selfishly or otherwise, they wanted their daughter to lead a normal life, without ridicule from others for being different.

Dr Malloney entered Eileen's hospital room.

'Hello Eileen and Tomas. I bet you are both glad to be going home tomorrow?' Dr Malloney said, holding Eileen's medical file.

'I certainly am. I'll go crazy if I stare at these walls any longer,' Eileen said with a smile.

'I've been very impressed with your progress, Eileen. Not just the physical healing but also with the medication you've been taking. How do you feel?'

'I feel good. I don't have any cravings.' Eileen knew it was the answer Dr Malloney wanted to hear.

'Good. Here's another prescription for the next fortnight and for my own peace of mind, I just want to reiterate, no alcohol at all. Okay?

'I understand, thank you.' Eileen took the prescription, placing it in her handbag.

'Now, the main reason for my visit today is to discuss the potential operation to remove Josephine's extra, post-axial digits.' Dr Malloney motioned for both of them to sit on the bed. 'There are several surgical options available, and they all depend on the type of polydactyly. What I have found is that depending on severity, surgical intervention *can* occur whilst still a newborn, before heading home. Most surgery is definitely recommended within the first year of life. In

Josephine's case, I would be reluctant to do this for a little while, because her immune system and lung function needs to get stronger, having been born six weeks premature. Based on her progress, I would anticipate an operation taking place between nine and twelve months of age.'

'Can it be done sooner if her progress is better than expected?' Eileen blurted out.

'Yes, it can, but let's take it one step at a time. Getting you home and settled before Josephine arrives, hopefully this time next week, is the first hurdle. Please call me any time if you have questions. I wish you both the very best as new parents.' Dr Malloney smiled and shook hands with each of them before she left the room.

With a sigh, Tomas got up and walked to the window. 'This isn't how I expected any of this to go.' He looked out through the glass pane into the world.

Eileen started to sob. 'I'm so sorry. This is all my fault.'

Tomas rushed over and embraced her as she completely broke down. 'Hey, it's okay. We'll get through this together,' Tomas said, wiping her tears with his handkerchief. 'I will admit, when Dr Malloney first told me about Josephine's extra digits and what might have caused them, I was angry and upset with the situation, with you.'

Eileen listened dejectedly as Tomas continued.

'We have a second chance now to fix our short comings. We can get you better, and Josephine can have an operation,' Tomas said, reassuringly. 'I understand why you want to blame yourself, but what's done is done. Let's not dwell on the past. Now, I have a few more things to do around the house in preparation for your homecoming, so I'll leave you be.' He kissed her on the forehead while cupping her face in his hands. Eileen smiled genuinely.

After Tomas left, Eileen sat for a moment on the bed in quiet reflection before she resumed packing her bag, ready for discharge the following morning. Grabbing the Diazepam packet, she gave herself a long hard stare in the mirror. She noticed her hair was lank, lifeless and brittle. Her eyes, once a vibrant green, had turned grey and dull. Pinching the prematurely withered and wrinkled skin on her cheek, she barely remembered when it was soft and subtle. Slowly but surely, the reflection morphed into the woman she was; deceitful, secretive, raising a bottle to her lips. The shape of a woman with long black hair stepped out from behind her, as if it were her shadow moving independently. Shrieking, she turned away from the mirror, dropping the medication on the floor.

'Am I going crazy? Who the hell was that?'

She checked her hands, half expecting to see a bottle. Suddenly frantic, she got down on her hands and knees and located the Diazepam packet under the bed. As she reached for it, she saw a pair of dirty, shoeless feet on the other side of the bed. Covering her mouth in an attempt to muffle her scream, she whimpered as she slowly and silently reversed her crawl. *I need a weapon.* But there was nothing at floor level for her to grab, only the Diazepam packet. Her heart was pounding, and she could feel her gut filling with nervous tension. Plucking up the courage, she decided to jump up and surprise whoever had wandered into her room. With palms flat to the floor, she pulled her legs in toward her torso and jumped.

'Oh, bloody hell. Jesus Christ that hurt.' Eileen yelled out in pain as she returned abruptly to the floor, after hitting her head on the bed frame.

Convinced she had given away her position, she cautiously got to her feet, raising the hand holding the medication above her while the other rubbed her sore head. There was nobody else in the room. Grabbing a glass of water from her side table, she took a double dose of pills before gingerly returning to face the mirror. The reflection was hers again, but that unsettled her all the more.

'Who am I?'

* * *

Tomas had a welcome home party to organise. He knew his wife wasn't keen on surprises, but after the news they had received about Josephine, he decided to focus on the positives, and sharing the joy of her arrival with friends and family simply had to happen. Invitations were made and sent, and everyone was sworn to secrecy.

One week later, Josephine was discharged as planned.

Chapter Ten

Homecoming

Arriving home with a baby was harder than Eileen expected. It felt as if she were returning to her old life, which part of her desperately wanted to leave behind. As Tomas opened the door to help her out of the truck, she sat staring straight ahead with a grimace on her face.

'It'll be okay, Eileen. This is a new beginning. The slate has been wiped clean and we have a second chance.' Tomas extended his hand. Eileen hesitated for a moment, then nervously took it and exited the vehicle clutching Josephine's hospital bag. Tomas reached in and gently retrieved their sleeping daughter, and together they made their way inside.

As soon as the front door opened, a chorus of hushed surprise rang out from the guests who had gathered. Eileen felt like running in the opposite direction. Sensing her apprehension, Tomas tenderly placed his hand on her back as they made their way to the sofa, which party guests quickly vacated. In attendance was William, who greeted her with a hug and a kiss and whispered in her ear that he had been sworn to secrecy. Eileen smiled and nodded in appreciation. Also present was her younger sister, Geraldine Ellis-Baxter, who had loosely been in contact with her during her pregnancy but who had recently been out of town on business. She was a fashion consultant for Pierre Cardin, and she travelled a lot, promoting the latest line of thigh-high boots, collarless jackets and Ormini dresses in bright colours. Her brother, Henry, was also there, sporting an unkept beard and wearing a jacket that looked remarkably like one she knew her father owned.

Following their embrace, Eileen ran her hands down the front of his jacket and said, 'Is this –'

'Yes, it's Dad's. I borrowed it for the event,' Henry admitted.

'It's really good to see you, Henry.' Eileen smiled and hugged him again.

Henry was currently unemployed. The economic downturn and political uncertainty had caused his employer to retrench most staff in the machinery business he'd worked for. He received a modest severance package as a long-standing employee. The question was how long he could make it last. Henry had occasionally assisted Tomas with the stock and various machinery issues, but as Tomas couldn't afford to pay him, he continued to look for paid employment elsewhere.

After several hours chatting with guests, mostly about Josephine and other associated baby stuff, Eileen excused herself to feed her daughter and then collapsed on the bed. She was tired, but also nervous about what lay ahead. She knew the routine she had been accustomed to would be changed forever. After her feed, Josephine was passed around the group for cuddles, with Geraldine and Henry taking to their aunty and uncle roles perfectly. Swallowing the medication Dr Malloney had prescribed, Eileen closed her eyes and fell asleep.

When she woke, several hours later, the house was quiet. After putting on her dusty-pink, rayon night-gown, she made her way to the nursery, where Josephine was fast asleep in her cot. She was loath to wake her, but the nurse at the hospital had told her, regular feeding would establish a pattern of sleep behaviour, making it easier for everyone. Eileen was grateful Josephine fed and slept well as she had a lot of growing to do. Eileen could hear commotion in the kitchen, and she put Josephine back in her cot.

'Tomas, is that you?'

'No, it's Geraldine. I'm sorry. Did I wake you?'

'No, not at all. You didn't have to stay,' Eileen said, yawning as she reached for the kettle to make a cup of tea.

'I wanted to. As it turned out, I had a couple of days leave owing to me, and when I heard about the early arrival of my niece, I simply couldn't imagine being anywhere else. I'm staying with Dad.'

'He'll be glad for the company in that big old house.'

'How are you doing? I know we've been out of touch lately, and I noticed Josephine's extra-.'

'Digits, yes. Things have been rather hectic here, and Tomas and I didn't get a chance to tell the entire family about it.' Eileen's tone was snappy.

'I'm sorry. I didn't mean to pry. Did the doctor tell you what might have caused it?'

Eileen was about to answer honestly when a little voice in her head said, *Lie. Get her on side. She can run to town for you to acquire what you've gone so long without.*

'Umm, yes. They said something about environmental considerations, genetic factors. Chemical exposure I think was mentioned too. Most of it went over my head. They really couldn't pinpoint exactly. When she is about nine months, she'll have them surgically removed and it will be as if they were never there. Hey, can I ask a favour?'

Geraldine was more than happy to help Eileen in any way she could and agreed to pop into town to collect what she had asked for. After all, running errands was all part of being an aunty, and she understood all too well the desire to keep a man happy with his favourite beverage as a reward at the end of a long, hard day. Eileen wasn't big on surprises, but she certainly knew how to keep a secret safe. She gave Geraldine only enough information to get the job done, and no more.

'Wow, Geraldine, you've really stepped up in the world,' Eileen spluttered enviously as she walked her sister out the back door to where her magnificently suave vehicle was parked.

Geraldine's husband, Claymore Baxter, was the typical tall, dark and handsome type. He had broad shoulders, neat, short black hair and ice-blue eyes. He managed the local Chevrolet plant and oversaw world-wide distribution of its vehicles. He had recently acquired a 1957 Chevrolet Bel Air convertible. She was a beautiful piece of machinery: two-tone mint green with polished chrome trim and rims. The vehicle glistened in the afternoon sun like a shiny new pearl, so much so you could clearly see your face in the duco. Eileen didn't think much of the reflection she saw and took a step back to spare herself the reality of her appearance, and to enhance the illusion she was admiring the car.

'Claymore thought it was about time we upgraded, and he was able to get considerable staff discount. Now, don't worry, I shall be back in about an hour with everything you've asked for.'

Geraldine turned the key and the engine purred to life. Giving Eileen a wave, she released her perfectly coiffed blonde hair, which proceeded to dance in the crisp air, along with her salmon-pink silk neck scarf, as she tore off down the road.

Eileen returned the wave half-heartedly, and jealously muttered, 'Bitch' as she turned to go back inside.

* * *

With Tomas managing the ranch, and Hosea's time split between running errands for her and helping her husband, Eileen had succumbed to post-natal depression. Geraldine's enthusiasm to help had restarted the chain of events that was to follow. The reflection in the mirror, first apparent in the hospital after Josephine was born, was now the only reflection Eileen saw. Her tired and frayed-at-the-edges appearance, with blood-shot eyes and greying hair, was normal, or so she thought, for a first-time mum.

The Arrabidine and Rectified Spirits helped her get through her days as she juggled her daughter's needs and that of the ranch. The medication she was taking initially made her sick when she drank, but she knew if she didn't take it Dr

Malloney, and eventually Tomas, would get suspicious. She'd experimented and found a way to balance her intake of drugs and alcohol to minimise the side effects, keeping everyone happy in the process.

The house, however, was a total mess, and nothing seemed to improve, regardless of how much effort she expended to get things done. There seemed to be endless washing, folding, mending and ironing, as well as cooking and cleaning. Barely holding it all together, some days she just wanted to close her eyes and never wake up again.

Chapter Eleven

Surgery

Nine months later, the day of Josephine's operation arrived.

'Hey, baby girl. We're going for a little ride, and when we come home again, this little pinky and that little pinky will be gone,' Tomas said, enthusiastically.

Josephine gazed into her daddy's eyes. She waved her extremities in the air, thinking he was playing with her, and she proceeded to giggle.

'Tomas, I can't find her socks and pacifier, damn it.' Eileen frantically searched the living room, casting another stack of clothes skyward in search of the misplaced items.

'Let me have a look, sweetheart. You place Josephine in the truck and I'll join you both shortly,' Tomas said, giving her a kiss.

After five minutes, Tomas came bounding out the front door waving Josephine's favourite pink socks and pacifier above his head. Eileen was relieved. Tomas was a great hands-on father, and nothing was too much trouble. Whilst she didn't need any more stress to deal with, he loved to be busy and appeared to thrive on it.

Dr Malloney was waiting for them in the paediatric ward of the Louisville County Hospital.

'Sorry to keep you waiting, Dr Malloney. We had some

issues,' Eileen said, as Tomas rounded the corner with their daughter.

'No need to apologise, Eileen. I understand the demands children place on parents, and how time goes out the window when that happens. How are you? You look a little tired and pale.'

'I'm fine. Sleep is for the single and unencumbered.'

Based on that remark, Dr Malloney made a mental note to pass on some post-natal depression material and contact information to Tomas after Josephine's operation, as she feared Eileen was already gripped by it.

'Please join me in my office for a moment, so I can run you both through what will happen this afternoon. Firstly, I need to ask, when did Josephine have her last feed?'

'About four hours ago, as per your instructions last week,' Tomas said.

'That's good. It reduces the chances of vomiting under anaesthesia, and after the operation as well.'

There was a knock on the office door.

'Come in.'

The door slowly opened and in walked a very tall, thin man with glasses. A blue cap covered his head to contain his hair and he wore a white coat. Behind his back he was holding a large two-tone teddy bear.

'Mr and Mrs Hubbard, this is Dr Edward Lewisham, the anaesthetist assisting me with the operation today,' Dr Malloney said.

'Hello. It's a pleasure to meet you both, and Josephine,

this little fella is for you.' He handed her the teddy, which she grabbed hold of and cuddled.

'The teddy, we find, helps children relax and it's important that it be shown to them again when they wake, to provide a sense of security and reassurance. We allow the teddy to remain with the child until they are under the anaesthesia, and then it is given to the parents to mind until the child is in recovery,' Dr Malloney explained.

'Now, we need to give Josephine some medication before the anaesthetic. It will help her relax, and it will also have a pain-relieving effect when the cannula is placed in her hand, through which the anaesthetic will be administered. It tastes like banana,' Dr Lewisham said.

He took a seat next to Tomas and Josephine and made the sound of a choo choo train until Josephine opened her mouth and swallowed the scented liquid.

Eileen laughed when her daughter screwed up her face, the new taste sensation apparently not to her liking.

'Dr Malloney, I have a question about the anaesthetic.'

'Certainly, Eileen. What is it?'

'As this is Josephine's first operation under a general anaesthetic, how do you know how much to give her?'

'That's a good question. For all patients we conduct a thorough review of their medical history, checking for any known issues that could impact the effectiveness of the anaesthetic, or that could cause complications during the operation. In Josephine's case, she is healthy with no underlying medical conditions. We weigh Josephine to ensure correct dosage, taking into account the anticipated length of the procedure. There is an educated best-guess approach involved as well.'

'So, what happens if she wakes mid-operation?' Eileen said, concerned.

'That would be extremely rare. However, if that did happen, I would put a little mask over her nose and mouth and she would gently breath in anaesthetic gas to remain under,' Dr Lewisham said, reassuringly.

There was another knock at the door. A nurse stuck her head in to let them know they were ready in theatre.

'Okay. Let's go.' Dr Lewisham began to move towards the door.

Josephine was already looking a little sleepy, indicating the medication had taken effect. The short walk to theatre allowed Dr Malloney to observe how Tomas and Eileen were interacting with Josephine and each other. She made more mental notes for later.

'This is Nurse Sullivan. She will be assisting in theatre today,' Dr Lewisham said, as he introduced her to the Hubbard's.

'Yes, we know each other. Nine months ago she helped deliver Josephine,' Tomas proudly declared.

'It's nice to see you all again, and look how much you've grown, Josephine. It's great to see she's done so well.' Nurse Sullivan gently touched the side of her little sleepy face.

'We need to weigh Josephine, so if you could place her on the scales, please, Tomas. Eileen you are welcome to wait next to the trolley,' Dr Lewisham said, while Dr Malloney and Nurse Sullivan scrubbed in.

Within thirty seconds of the cannula being inserted, Josephine was fast asleep and was transferred onto the operating table. Tomas took the teddy, her pacifier and her little pink socks as they were handed to him.

'The operation will take about four hours. If you wish to stay, you can wait in the recovery ward waiting room, just down the hall to your right. There is a small cafeteria there, with a range of food and drinks. Nurse Sullivan will inform you when you are able to see her Josephine again. She'll be fine. Try not to worry,' Dr Malloney added, since Eileen's concerned expression hadn't changed much since walking through the door an hour or so earlier.

The next four hours felt like eight. Eileen seemed relaxed, flicking through several magazines on the comfy, tan-coloured sofa in the corner of the cafeteria. She was enjoying, in her own way, the time away from having to be a constantly attentive mother. Tomas struggled to settle though and paced.

'Darling, would you sit down. You're driving me insane. Just relax,' Eileen said, in an agitated tone.

'Sorry, sweetheart. I can't help but worry. She's our little girl. Aren't you worried?'

'Not really. She's in the best of care, and Dr Malloney allayed my fears in answering the questions I had earlier. There's nothing we can do, so why get worried about it?'

'You're right. I'll sit over here and read. Can I get you anything whilst I'm up?'

'No, thank you,' Eileen replied with a forced, slivered smile.

Tomas decided it would be best for him to sit out of sight. He was aware of the stress Eileen was under, and he wanted to have a private word with Dr Malloney when he got the chance.

Four and a half hours passed before Nurse Sullivan entered the waiting room.

'Mr and Mrs Hubbard, the operation is complete. It all went according to plan and there were no complications. She is now in the recovery ward. Please follow me.'

After a short walk down the corridor, they entered a darkened room where it took a moment for their eyes to adjust. Josephine was asleep and looked so peaceful and tiny in the enormous white bed. Tomas placed the teddy alongside her, observing her hands were completely enveloped in bandages, as were her feet. Eileen sat next to the head of the bed and began gently stroking her hair. Tomas took advantage of the moment to pull Dr Malloney aside for a quick word.

'Dr Malloney, thank you. I understand it all went very well. My concern isn't for Josephine, however.'

'Please, let's step outside. Is this about Eileen?'

'Yes.'

'I'm glad you've noticed, as I picked up on a few verbal and non-verbal clues earlier. I believe she may be suffering from post-natal depression.'

'How do we deal with it?'

'Do you know if she's still drinking? She will be very good at hiding it and will deny it emphatically if you confront her about it.'

'If I'm honest, I have to say I don't know. I'm gone from the house most of the day, managing the ranch. I can't constantly watch her.'

'Okay. I'm going to give you some post-natal depression reading material and contact information. I want you to leave it out somewhere where she will come across it. If we passively try to introduce it to her, she won't feel as threatened by it. Also, if you could vary your routine a little. For example, get back to the house early for lunch some days, or knock off early. She will have a routine, too, and if she is drinking you may be able to catch her out. However, all I want you to do is report back to me and not confront her about it. Let me deal with it on a professional level. I'm reluctant to give her more medication at this stage. It might react badly with the alcohol withdrawal medication she's been taking. I shall have to do some research first.'

'But isn't the medication she's been taking supposed to make her ill if she drinks?'

'Yes, but I suspect she has experimented with her intake of alcohol, to limit the side effects. For most people, the medication enables them to break free of alcohol addiction but for some it doesn't. Also, perhaps surprise her with flowers or offer to cook dinner. Go out and see a movie and get her sister to babysit for a night here and there. Raising children is a joint effort. If one parent feels the other isn't pulling their weight, perceived or otherwise, there will be tension,' Dr Malloney said, just before Eileen suddenly joined them in the corridor.

'What are you two whispering about?'

'Just going over the details of the surgery, sweetheart,' Tomas said in quick reply.

'Josephine will stay in hospital for a couple of days, just so we can monitor her and watch for any post-operative tummy upset as the anaesthetic works its way out of her system. The spare bed next to hers is for a parent if you want to take it in turns to stay with her. The bandages on her hands and feet will have to be replaced daily for the first week or so. We shall arrange for a nurse to visit you at your home, rather than you having to drive in for that,' Dr Malloney explained.

'How long will the bandages need to stay on for?' Eileen asked, apparently having bought Tomas' lie.

'For at least the next two weeks. After that we will assess the healing process before we decide further. When you return home, I want you to let me know immediately if she is ill or has a temperature, as it could indicate an infection that would require antibiotics. Now, I have a couple of other patients to see on my rounds, so go in there and spend some quality time together as a family.' Dr Malloney smiled before she headed down the corridor and out of sight.

* * *

Josephine's operation had been a huge success. Four little scars were the only physical reminder there was ever an issue. By the age of two, she was a little slower at learning to speak, her hand-eye coordination was under-developed and she was small for a child of her age, but she was making progress.

* * *

Eileen, like many mothers before her, had been told that sleep deprivation would come with the territory once Josephine came into the world. Like most, she'd underestimated what sleep deprivation meant and just how little she'd get. What she struggled with more so was the reconciliation of the strange dreams she'd been having since Josephine's birth. Some she'd remember vividly the following morning and mull over the meaning of them throughout her day. Others were vague, disjointed, muddled and impossible to make any sense of. Equally, she found them all unsettling.

Several weeks out from her thirty-fourth birthday, she recalled one particularly disturbing night terror. It started out as a beautiful and pleasant afternoon with the family, on holiday, at the beach. Gradually the wind picked up and clouds thickened on the horizon – a storm was brewing. Wanting just another five more minutes of sun, she closed her eyes, but instead fell into a deep sleep. Distant screams got louder and louder until she woke to hear her husband's unusually strained voice urging her to get up and move. What she heard was unsettling enough but when she sat bolt upright and removed her sunglasses, what she saw terrified her. The clouds were churning above her, blood red and flame yellow, her skin was prickling, the hair on her forearms melted and disintegrated. She felt her eyebrows and eyelashes were doing the same.

Tomas tugged at her arm with increasing intensity, and as he lost his grip and fell, she woke up profusely sweating, heart racing and alone.

Tomas had gotten up before dawn to start his day and his side of the bed was stone cold. Bed clothes littered the floor as Eileen flung her legs over the side of the bed and rolled out looking and feeling dishevelled. Staggering to the nursery to check on Josephine, she found her asleep and decided not to wake her for a feed. Peace and quiet was hard to come by, even if it was for just an extra minute or two. She feared losing her sanity entirely. She returned to the bedroom, with the intent of getting some more sleep, but stood aghast in the doorway, her eyes fixated on the bed. A black outline of where she'd been laying clearly visible. Cautiously she approached, unsure of what to make of it. As she touched the outline, looked at her fingers and rose them to her nose, the black and grey substance smelled like ash – but how could that be? She rubbed her arms and checked her eyebrows in the mirror. A momentary sense of relief washed over her.

Turning back towards the bed, her dream came rushing back – the same atmospheric burning smell now flooded her nostrils. Josephine had begun to stir but Eileen didn't hear her. The roar inside her head drowned out any other sound. She was alone on the debris-strewn beach. Abandoned chairs, picnic baskets, umbrellas and towels were dancing chaotically in the wind as sand stung her ankles. She strained to look in the direction of the car park, but her vehicle was nowhere to be seen. *Thomas left me here?* Feeling increasingly anxious, Eileen began to head in that direction, all the while fighting against the elements and discarded items as they flew around and crashed into her. She started to scream out Tomas' name in the hope he'd hear her even though she had no idea where he was.

Tomas was on his way back to the house for his morning cuppa when he heard his name and rushed inside to see Josephine sitting in the middle of the living room floor. He picked her up and together they stood in the doorway of the bedroom observing Eileen, apparently in a trance, moving awkwardly against some invisible force as she continued to periodically scream his name.

Tomas didn't know what to do. Josephine, who'd been getting increasingly anxious listening to and now observing the situation screamed; 'Mummy, stop it!'

Eileen turned in the direction of the sound just as a chair from her daydream hit her and she fell backwards onto the bed, snapping out of her trance-like state.

'Tomas, what happened?' Eileen asked, as she sat up rubbing her shoulder where the chair had impacted her.

'You're asking me? You were screaming out my name, waving your arms around and staggering like you were being attacked by a swarm of bees or something.

'Was I? Hmm, I was at the beach and there was a storm and I couldn't find you. It felt so…real. I can still feel the sand stinging my ankles.' She said, rubbing them.

It was the most intense dream Eileen had experienced and Constance enjoyed basking in the anxiety and confusion it had caused.

Chapter Twelve

Sparks

As another year rolled around, Eileen would have preferred the number associated with the age she was about to turn be less than it was, and she certainly didn't want to celebrate. Tomas had other ideas, however, and had colluded with the neighbour's wife to bake a Pineapple Upside Down Cake, complete with thirty-four candles. It was Eileen's favourite dessert. At the end of the meal, Tomas cleared the dishes and retrieved the cake from its hiding spot in the pantry. Josephine must have sensed something special was about to happen because she became excited and started rocking the highchair, which drew Eileen's attention. Tomas seized upon the moment and presented the cake, along with a box of matches.

'Aww, Tomas, you're a naughty man. My favourite dessert. Did Elsie make this?'

'She did indeed. Upon request. You can thank her personally in a minute as I invited her and Geoff to stop by.'

Moments later a car pulled into the driveway, and Elsie and Geoff made their way to the front door.

It was a mild night with a light breeze blowing gently from the south-east.

Elsie was about to knock on the front door when a cold shiver ran the length of her spine. She froze.

'What is it, darling? Are you alright?' Geoff enquired.

'I don't know. Something doesn't feel right, but you know me and my overactive imagination,' Elsie replied, trying to diffuse the incident so her husband didn't worry further.

Elsie stepped back and Geoff, still looking in his wife's direction, moved forward and knocked.

Shortly afterwards, Tomas opened the door. 'Hello Geoff, good to see you.' They shook hands. 'Where's Elsie?'

'She's right behind me,' Geoff commented, as she stepped into view, putting on a happy relaxed face.

'Elsie, thank you so much. Eileen's just lighting the candles now.' They hugged, and Elsie presented him with a tub of ice cream. 'Perfect. Please come in.'

Two steps in the door, as Tomas hung their coats on the rack, an eruption of flame engulfed the remaining unlit candles on the cake and ignited them. Josephine, usually mesmerised and relaxed by the sight of fire, sat completely still and could only point at the cake with her mouth wide open. Eileen was frantically rubbing her face and checking her hair and eyebrows after pushing her chair away from the table.

'Whoa. Clearly a little too much alcohol in the glaze there, Elsie,' Tomas remarked as they all began to sing 'Happy Birthday'. He then headed to the kitchen to gather tea and coffee cups and plates for the cake and ice cream. Geoff offered his assistance and joined him.

Elsie was just as stunned as Eileen when their eyes met and the cold shiver returned. There was no alcohol in the glaze.

There was nothing flammable whatsoever, to have caused that reaction.

* * *

It was now mid-winter 1963. The average temperature during the day hovered around thirty-seven degrees Fahrenheit. The wind whistled through the long-leafed pines and deciduous black birch trees that ran the length of the northern fence line behind the Hubbard homestead. The combustion fire had been burning constantly for the past week to help keep the place warm and firewood reserves were getting low. Tomas had spent the best part of his week tending to the stock, as he had lost a few head of cattle to the cold. He and Hosea took it in turns to rotate them through the extreme weather shelter, as not all of them could be housed at one time.

With Josephine settled in her cot in the living room, Eileen decided to place another couple of logs in the combustion stove, before pouring herself her third drink for the afternoon. To warm up, she decided to take a nice long, hot shower. Twenty minutes later, the logs in the combustion stove were well alight and had become unbalanced. As she opened the bathroom door, drink in hand, hair wrapped tightly in a towel, the steam that had built up billowed out into the living room. The vibration caused the logs in the combustion stove to collapse, sending out a plethora of sparks. Eileen shrieked as some of them danced in the air, making their way towards her dusty-pink, rayon night-gown, which she understood was flammable.

What she hadn't realised was that a spark had ignited the remainder of her drink before she skulled the rest of it. The flammable liquid and rush of accompanying air set alight the alcohol she had already consumed, prior to her shower. A moment of panic overtook her as she realised her concerns about her night-gown were suddenly the least of her worries. She coughed, and a ball of blue flame exited her mouth, after which her airway constricted so she could no longer breathe, speak or scream. Clawing at her throat in a vain attempt to open her flash-burned airway, she collapsed in the bathroom doorway mere metres from Josephine, who stared at her from her cot across the room.

Writhing in pain, she eventually vomited the contents of her stomach, which set her ablaze. The logs in the combustion stove moved again, releasing another small volume of sparks. This time, however, they didn't aimlessly dance in the air; they headed directly for Josephine. Upon reaching her cot, they formed a rotating circle above her.

Fascinated by the sight of the tiny, glowing balls of light, Josephine extended her hand to touch them, but they instantly extinguished. It was the last surprising and yet horrifying thing Eileen saw, as her own life was, at that moment, also extinguished.

Tomas was making his way toward the house after rotating the last of the stock through the extreme weather shelter for the day when he heard Josephine's cries. Instantly picking up the pace, he opened the front door and smoke billowed out.

Shit. The place is on fire.

'Eileen! Eileen!' he yelled, as he grabbed Josephine out of her cot, covering her face and keeping low to the ground.

Eileen didn't respond.

Looking immediately at the combustion stove, he determined initially that the flue had backed up and let the room fill with smoke, as it was otherwise intact. But as the haze began to clear through the open front door, he saw his wife's motionless and flaming body in the bathroom doorway.

Panicked, he rushed Josephine into the kitchen, which had the least amount of smoke, and placed her on the floor. Then, after urgently filling a bucket with water, he raced over and threw it on his wife. There was no reaction. He realised he was moments too late to save her. He attempted to cradle her, but the heat radiating from her body meant he could not get close for long. The smell of burned flesh was nauseating. He knew he had to tend to his daughter and get her out into some fresh air. Through emotion thicker than the smoke, he wailed to Hosea, who was still in the extreme weather shelter, to urgently come to the house.

Hosea was battling with an uncooperative bull when he heard Tomas. The raised, stressed tone of his voice made the hair on the back of his neck stand up as he ran toward the house. When he arrived, Tomas was on the front porch holding Josephine in his arms, tears streaming down his face.

'Tomas, what's wrong? Why are you and Josephine covered in –.'

'I got back to the house and, oh God, - it was full of smoke. I grabbed Josephine and called … called out for Eileen. She … didn't answer me. When the smoke cleared I saw … Eileen's dead, Hosea.'

The look of disbelief and shock on Hosea's face spoke volumes as he embraced Tomas and Josephine. He then tried to enter the premises, but Tomas blocked his path.

'Please. It's better if you don't see. I need to call the police.'

'What can I do, Tomas? Hosea tried hard to keep his own emotions in check.

'Can you look after Josephine, while I wait for the police? Please take her to the hospital for me? Explain who you are, and who you work for, and get them to assess her for smoke inhalation. Ask for Nurse Sullivan if she's on duty, as she delivered Josephine and knows who we are.'

'Certainly, Tomas. I will take care of her as if she were my own.' Hosea immediately strapped Josephine into the truck and left.

When the police arrived, Tomas prepared to explain what he thought had happened.

'Mr Hubbard, is it?' the sergeant said, extending his hand. 'I'm Sergeant Horace Edgecombe and this is Constable Aron Eckersley. I understand this is a very emotional time for you and I'm sorry for your loss. To the best of your knowledge, can you tell us what happened here this afternoon?'

With his hands deep in his pockets, a visibly upset Tomas began.

'Thank you. Umm, sure. I'll try. My ranch hand, Hosea

Jackson, and I spent most of the day down in the extreme weather shelter, tending to the stock as we have done all week. My wife, Eileen, was in the house with our daughter, Josephine. I was returning to the house, leaving Hosea to finish up with the last of the stock, when I heard Josephine crying. I opened the front door and received a face full of smoke. I immediately made my way to Josephine and called out for Eileen, only there was no answer. I left the front door open as I entered. Once the smoke cleared, I saw my wife motionless and on fire in the bathroom doorway. I didn't know if she was …. - if it was already too late. I rushed into the kitchen, filled a bucket with water and threw it on her, but got no reaction.'

'Please, take your time, Mr Hubbard. Where is your daughter now?'

'I asked Hosea to take her to the hospital to be assessed for smoke inhalation. She's only two.'

'Okay, Mr Hubbard. We'll need to speak with Hosea when he returns from the hospital. If we're still here then, we'll catch him. Otherwise here are our details to arrange a time to get his statement,' Sergeant Edgecombe said.

'Do you have any idea how the fire might have started?' Constable Eckersley enquired.

'No, I'm sorry, I don't. When I saw Eileen on fire, all I could think about was smothering the flames. We have always been so careful around the fire with a toddler in the house, and I'm lost for any other explanation.'

'Are there any next of kin who need to be notified?'

'Yes, her father, William Ellis, her sister, Geraldine Ellis-

Baxter and brother, Henry Ellis. I'll give you their contact details.'

Tomas headed toward the bedroom to retrieve the address book as the police continued to note their observations of the scene, awaiting the arrival of the forensic pathologist.

* * *

Hosea pulled the truck up to the front entrance of the Louisville County Hospital, jumped out and began to unstrap Josephine from the vehicle. A white security guard on duty approached hastily.

'Hey buffie, whose truck and child is this?' he said, in an accusatory tone, tapping his baton numerous times on the truck's bonnet.

Hosea stopped what he was doing and immediately turned so his back was against the truck door. 'Sir, umm, I work for Tomas Hubbard. The truck is his, and this is his daughter. There's been a fire at the property and she needs to be assessed for smoke inhalation. Please let me pass,' Hosea pleaded. Josephine started to cough and was rubbing her eyes.

The guard continued to inspect the vehicle. He retrieved and read the registration papers tucked behind the sun visor. 'Hmmm, very well.

Hosea unbuckled Josephine and scurried to the reception desk.

'Excuse me, my name is Hosea Jackson. I work for Mr

Tomas Hubbard, and this is his daughter, Josephine. Is Nurse Sullivan available? She knows the family.'

'Where is Mr Hubbard?' the receptionist replied, peering over her glasses whilst looking Hosea up and down.

'There's been a fire at the farm and he is with the police. Please, my concern is for Josephine, not myself. Is Nurse Sullivan available?' Hosea repeated.

'Okay. Wait here and I'll find out for you.'

A few moments later the receptionist reappeared, followed by a nurse.

'Hello Mr Jackson, I'm Nurse Sullivan. Please follow me, quickly.'

Chapter Thirteen

Aftermath

U pon arrival at the Hubbard residence, Dr Strickland, the forensic pathologist (now a thirty-year veteran), began photographing the scene before anyone else trampled through the evidence. He asked if there were any witnesses to what had happened. Tomas indicated, that, to the best of his knowledge, no-one was present other than his two-year-old daughter. Dr Strickland noted every detail. The combustion stove in the kitchen was alight, but contained only a few glowing coals in the bottom. This indicated it must have been roaring a few hours earlier. The door was closed, the flue undamaged and it appeared intact. He would have to have someone check for any internal blockages, though before he ruled it out as a cause. Smashed glass was located at its base with a faint smell of alcohol still present on some fragments.

She was drinking when this happened, I must find the bottle.

The plastic, sunflower-patterned shower curtain over the bath had partially melted from the radiant heat. It appeared, from the lack of clothing on Eileen's body, she had just gotten out of the shower when the fire occurred. Fire damage was mainly contained to the front of her body; the abdomen, stomach, chest, neck and jaw. The towel encompassing her hair had survived the fire as it had been moist. A closer internal inspection would be conducted back at the morgue. Uncharacteristically, both eyes were wide open, and judging by the angle of her head, she was looking in the direction of Josephine's soot-covered cot. Eileen's right arm was also fully extended in that direction. Her last thoughts had been of her child, Dr Strickland surmised. The bathroom ceiling was dripping condensation, indicating both the external window and internal door had been closed.

Once he'd completed his initial assessment of the scene, Dr Strickland and made his way to where police were questioning Mr Hubbard.

'Constable. I'm sorry, but may I interrupt?' Dr Strickland asked.

The constable nodded, and removed himself from the immediate vicinity to allow them to talk.

'Mr Hubbard, I'm Dr Marcus Strickland. I'm very sorry for your loss this evening. I just have a couple of questions, if you don't mind, before we remove your wife's body for autopsy, to determine cause of death.'

Through bloodshot and teary eyes, Tomas looked in the direction of his recently deceased wife before lowering his head and indicating for Strickland to proceed.

'Can I ask you how old your wife was, Mr Hubbard?'

'We'd just celebrated her thirty-fourth birthday last month.' Tomas wrapped his arms around himself for comfort.

'I see. And do you have any alcohol in the house?'

'No, we don't. My wife wasn't allowed to drink. She was

taking medication to deal with –.'

'I'm sorry, Mr Hubbard. You were saying?'

'Umm, sorry, yes. Medication to deal with alcohol-with-drawal symptoms.'

'Do you drink, Mr Hubbard?'

'No, I never have.'

'I found a broken glass near the combustion stove, and indication there was alcohol in it. If you find the bottle from which it came, could you let me know?' Dr Strickland said, handing him his business card.

'Sure. Certainly.' Tomas felt the knife twist in his chest a little more at the thought, his wife had been deceitful again and presumably for some time.

'Thank you, Mr Hubbard. That's all the questions I have for now. I will be in touch if I have further questions and when I have the autopsy results, which will take a few days,' Dr Strickland said, with a thin smile, placing a firm hand on his shoulder before they parted company.

Several hours later, everyone cleared out and Tomas was allowed back into his home. He immediately commenced searching for alcohol. Starting in the kitchen, he literally tore the place apart. The emotion of the night, his wife's deceit, the effort it took to run a ranch and keep a family moving forward was enough to turn a man to drink. Nothing! No evidence in the cupboards, trash receptacle or pantry of any bottles, not even empty ones. He checked the bathroom next and again found nothing. The living room and master bedroom also came up empty. Could the doctor have been wrong?

The only room remaining was Josephine's nursery. Standing in the doorway, he paused to remember the moment at the hospital when he'd first gazed upon his newborn daughter. The huge sense of pride he'd felt at becoming a father for the first time, and the instant love he'd felt towards her.

Again, his search was fruitless, and he collapsed on the floor emotionally drained. He grabbed one of his daughter's teddy bears, stared at it, and began to sob uncontrollably. Josephine would never get to know her mother, and Eileen would never get to see her daughter grow up, get married and hopefully have children of her own.

After several minutes, he composed himself and looked out into the living room to see Josephine's soot-covered cot. It was the one remaining place he hadn't searched, and it would be cruel and ironic if the evidence Dr Strickland needed was located there. He staggered to his feet. Through tear-soaked eyes, he discovered a three-quarters-empty bottle of Arrabidine hidden under the mattress, along with an almost-empty bottle of Rectified Spirits. Letting out an excruciating groan, Tomas did his best to adjudicate between relief at finding some evidence and the rage that was steadily building inside him. The desire to throw the bottles as far as he could was over-whelming, but then he remembered Dr Strickland's request.

Returning to the destroyed kitchen, Tomas located an unbroken mug amongst the debris scattered on the benchtop and made himself a herbal tea to quell his fury before calling Dr Strickland's office.

As Dr Strickland's assistants unloaded Eileen's body for autopsy, they mentioned it felt lighter than when they had loaded it into their vehicle at the Hubbard farm, a mere half an hour earlier. Initially, Dr Strickland thought the suggestion absurd, but when he unzipped the bag, he was astonished at what he saw. Eileen's body had indeed further disintegrated, with most features, though observed when photographed, now indistinguishable. It appeared her body had continued to smoulder during transportation; although, the vinyl bag containing the remains appeared unaffected. Tomas Hubbard had stated he'd thrown a large pale of water over her, which apparently had only extinguished the visible, external flame. An internal examination was now going to be very difficult indeed, as most of the corpse had been reduced to fatty ash sludge. Her jaw, neck, chest, ribcage, stomach, abdomen, pelvis and thighs were simply no longer in recognisable form to examine.

* * *

Half an hour after consuming his herbal tea, Tomas was calm enough to call Dr Strickland.

'Dr Strickland, please. This is Tomas Hubbard. He's expecting my call.' Tomas was blunt.

The secretary transferred the call, and after a momentary pause, Dr Strickland answered.

'Hello Mr Hubbard. How can I help?'

'You asked me to call if I found the alcohol bottle.'

'Ah, yes. There should be two different bottles, in fact,' Dr Strickland confirmed.

'Well, yes, I did find two, but how –'

'The preliminary testing on the glass fragments I found by your combustion stove indicated a liqueur called Arrabidine, and Rectified Spirits were in her system at the time she died.'

'That matches the bottles I found. Do you need them for testing?'

'No, not now you've confirmed the results. I also found Valium in her system, which I assume she was taking to combat the alcohol-withdrawal symptoms?'

'Yes. Dr Caroline Malloney prescribed it to replace Diazepam, which she had previously been taking for years.'

'Very well. I will prepare the full report over the next couple days and meet with you, in my office, to go through it. Oh, before I go, how is your daughter?'

'My ranch hand, Hosea, informed me from the hospital that she inhaled very little smoke. I got to her just in time.'

'That's good news, Mr Hubbard. We'll talk again soon,' Dr Strickland said, and hung up.

Staring down at the two bottles in his hand, Tomas could feel the rage slowly building in his gut again. His eyes glazed over and he launched them at the living room wall, one after the other. Then he collapsed on the soot-covered sofa and stared at the glass fragments and the residual liquid running down the wall.

Hosea, holding a sleeping Josephine, witnessed Tomas' moment of madness as he stood in the doorway upon returning from the hospital. Eileen had been so kind to him over the years. To see his friend and employer grief-stricken at the loss of his wife under such tragically inexplicable circumstances was emotionally shattering for him too. He made his way to the sofa and together they sat surveying the destruction in deafening silence.

Three days later …

Chapter Fourteen

Goodbye

William and Tomas sat side by side in Dr Strickland's office, staring at the wall behind his desk. It was adorned with his degree parchment, other certifications and awards. Gripped by grief, neither man took much in.

Dr Strickland entered and made his way to his desk.

'Sorry to keep you waiting, gentlemen. I wanted my secretary to make a copy of the report for both of you.' He handed a five-page document to each of them.

Tomas extended his arm on autopilot and clutched the document when he felt it hit his palm. William acknowledged receipt of his copy with a slivered smile and avoided direct eye contact.

'Now, I won't go through each page in detail. Rather, I wish to give you an overview of the contents. If you have any questions, please feel free to ask me as they arise. After reviewing the evidence at the scene that night, the photographs taken, and the autopsy results, I have concluded that Eileen died from SHC or Spontaneous Human Combustion —'

'Err, I'm sorry, but what did you just say?' William stammered.

'Spontaneous Human Combustion,' Dr Strickland repeated.

'Not again. It's not possible. Not my daughter as well!' William muttered.

Dr Strickland read his shocked expression, and from William's comment, he realised he was the brother of Margaret Ellis – his second case of SHC twenty-seven years earlier.

'Delores, get me the file on Margaret Cynthia Ellis, date of death 1936, from the archives immediately, please.' Dr Strickland was insistent as he bellowed through his intercom.

'Right away, sir,' came the reply.

The walls of Dr Strickland's office began to race towards William. Loosening his tie and undoing his top button, he indicated he needed some air and tried to stand, but stumbled. Tomas assisted him to the door and out into the corridor. Dr Strickland was still seated behind his desk flicking frantically through his paperwork. William's pale complexion and clammy skin alerted Tomas to call for him. As Dr Strickland joined them in the corridor, William slid down the wall into a crumpled heap. Dr Strickland called to a nearby assistant to fetch some water and a blanket as he knew William was going into shock. It was no surprise, considering the news he had just received. For Dr Strickland it was a finding that could set his career on a whole new path. For William, it could prematurely end his life.

* * *

Geraldine Ellis-Baxter had a great working relationship with her boss at Pierre Cardin. She had consistently been the company's top regional saleswoman for the last five years. She rarely took annual leave, so when she required some time off to plan her sister's funeral, it was granted unreservedly. Her father, William, and brother-in-law, Tomas, weren't coping well with the sudden loss of Eileen. They looked direction-less and withered, defeated by the hand life had dealt them. William had been prescribed some anti-depressants, and Tomas was barely going through the motions of caring for Josephine. Hosea had taken complete control of the ranch, so Geraldine took charge of organising the funeral, placing her own grief on hold.

The local Catholic priest, Father Dominic Pritchard, would preside over the service, like he'd done for both Berna-dette and Margaret's funerals decades earlier. When he heard of Eileen's passing, he was one of the first to telephone William to express his condolences and offer words of comfort.

Eileen's casket would be solid mahogany and lined with luxurious white velvet. In life, Eileen didn't have many luxuries, so Geraldine and Claymore made sure that in death, she did. A wreath of red roses, her favourite flower, with scattered white stargazer lilies was ordered to sit atop the casket. Guests attending the service would each receive a yellow rose, which they would be invited to place on the casket near the end of the service, to pay their respects. Eileen and Tomas weren't religious people, so the service would be simple in format, and afterwards there would be a gathering at the gravesite for the burial.

* * *

The day of the funeral arrived. Family and mourners trickled into the Louisville Catholic Church. After a welcome message from Father Pritchard, Geraldine read Psalm 23, which was followed by the congregation singing 'Amazing Grace'. When friends and family were invited to share their recollections of Eileen, Susan Staffordshire-Routledge made her way to the front and stood beside the casket.

'Eileen and I were the best of friends. I remember once when we both snuck out from our dorm after curfew to meet some boys and smoke cigarettes. We thought we were so cool and were convinced we had gotten away with it. Needless to say, our dorm mistress was waiting at the end of Eileen's bed when we returned. Our punishment for breaking the rules was dishes and bathroom clean-up for three months. I'll miss you, Eileen, and all the fun times we had.'

As Susan returned to her seat, William asked Geraldine who she was. Geraldine shrugged and said she had no idea. Eileen had never mentioned her. Even in death, Susan had a way of making it all about herself. It was all a blur for William and Tomas, and neither of them chose to speak. Father Pritchard then addressed the congregation.

'I wish to read a statement prepared by the family. Eileen was a kind and gentle soul, which became evident at a young age. After losing her mother, Bernadette, when she was just six, she stepped up and took charge of caring for her younger sister, Geraldine, and infant brother, Henry, as William and his sister Margaret, or Aunty Margie to the children, learned to deal with the loss. She enjoyed life on the ranch with her siblings and the lessons hardship taught her. Learning to be resourceful with the little the family had was a challenge she excelled at. She was always recycling used items and repurposing them. At the age of sixteen she fell off the family horse and was in a coma for three days. The love and devotion of her father, William, saw him keep vigil at her hospital bedside until she woke.

She was courted by a local rancher, Tomas Hubbard, and William recalls the night Tomas knocked on his door and asked for his daughter's hand in marriage. William and Tomas became close as they supported the needs of the extended family. There was never a prouder man when Eileen announced the news of her first pregnancy. William would become a grandfather to Josephine and Tomas a proud father. Eileen had her issues with alcohol addiction, which was no secret, but with the love and support of an understanding family, the burden was shared.'

A creaking pew broke the silence as Henry shifted awkwardly in his seat.

'Today we mourn the loss of a wife, mother, daughter, sister and friend. Cherish the memories and your loved ones. Don't let the sun go down on your anger, as tomorrow may never come. Regret can last a lifetime. It's time to say goodbye. Rest in peace with the angels, our beautiful Eileen.'

William blew his nose, and Geraldine placed her arm around his shoulder. Tomas was red-faced, Josephine beside him. She was swinging her legs and playing with her favourite teddy, oblivious to what was taking place.

As the organist commenced the hymn 'Nearer My God to Thee', Father Pritchard invited parishioners to attend the local cemetery for the committal of the body to the earth. After the hymn concluded, William and Geraldine exited the church arm in arm. Tomas and Josephine then followed.

At the base of the front steps William turned to Geraldine and said, 'It was a beautiful send off. Thank you for organising it all. I just couldn't see my way through the haze to do it.'

'Yes, it was, Dad.' She patted his forearm and wiped a tear from her cheek.

At the gravesite burial service, Geraldine spied a woman separate from the main group, and leant in to enquire of her father. 'Dad, see that woman dressed in black over your left shoulder, with the long black hair. Do you know who she is?'

William turned, trying not to be too obvious and responded, 'I've no idea. She can't be a local as I've never seen her before.'

Geraldine glanced again, but the mystery woman had vanished.

Chapter Fifteen

Pain

It was mid-summer 1965. Geraldine had just landed at Northwest Alabama Regional Airport after a whirlwind tour of Dallas and Houston to promote the latest line of ladies' fashion and accessories. She was exhausted. It was the first time she had celebrated a birthday away from her family in some time, and not being able to share it with her sister was playing heavily on her mind.

Prior to leaving Dallas, she had felt nauseated, with slight pain on her right-hand side. She had ignored it, putting it down to over-exertion after weeks of being on the go. It had abated during the flight but had now returned, and she crippled over in pain shortly after retrieving her belongings from the baggage carousel. A couple collecting their luggage nearby came to her aid, but not wanting to cause more of a scene, she played it down insisting she had only pulled a muscle as she collected her things, and then scurried away. However, something wasn't right and she believed she might be suffering from an acute attack of appendicitis. She made her way to the airport first aid station where a doctor was called for an assessment. She was then taken by ambulance to the Louisville County Hospital.

* * *

William could hear his phone ringing in the hall as he struggled to unlock his front door. Unfortunately, he didn't manage to pick it up before it ceased. He dialled 0 to speak with the operator.

'Operator, how may I direct your call?'

'Operator, I've just missed a call on this extension. Could you reconnect me?

'Certainly, Mr Ellis, one moment please.'

It was the Hospital informing him of his daughter Geraldine's condition. The doctor reported he believed it to be appendicitis and wanted his consent to operate. William gave it without hesitation. His bond with Geraldine had strengthened after the sudden loss of Eileen. William had been a non-drinker all his life. He was confident in the knowledge Geraldine was the same, but the operation still made him nervous. Margaret and Eileen had both died at thirty-four, now Geraldine was the same age. He made his way to the hospital, and waited patiently with Geraldine's husband, Claymore, and Henry for news on his daughter's condition.

After they'd paced the halls for several hours, consuming numerous cups of coffee, a doctor appeared at the waiting room door.

'Mr Baxter, Mr Ellis, Geraldine had a cyst on her liver, which has now been successfully removed. It will be sent to pathology for testing, but it isn't believed to be cancerous. She will be in hospital for a few days, to monitor for any post-operative infection. She's now in the Recovery Ward, and immediate family can go in and see her.'

After knocking on the Recovery Ward door, Claymore entered, and Geraldine slowly opened her sleepy eyes, managing a thin smile and extending her shaking hand toward him.

'Honey, you really gave us a scare there,' Claymore said, clutching her hand and adjusting her hair. 'Has anyone ever told you that you work too hard?'

'I might have heard that once or twice from a certain husband,' Geraldine slurred with a grin. Claymore then kissed her on the forehead.

'The good news is the doctor says you'll be fine, and you'll be out of here in a few days.'

Geraldine smiled again and shifted awkwardly, trying to get comfortable. Another knock at the door and William entered. This time Geraldine whispered, 'Daddy,' and began to cry as he made his way to the foot of the bed.

'Hey, pumpkin. Now, enough of that. We're all here and you'll be fine. Just rest and do as you're told, and you'll be home again before you know it,' William said, sternly but affectionately.

Another knock and Henry appeared at the door. William motioned for him to come in. He made his way to the head of the bed and kissed Geraldine's hand. He leant in and whispered in her ear, 'I'm sorry for everything, sis.' He smelled of a mix of alcohol and stale body odour. He was unshaven, but his hair was neat. William had insisted earlier he use some of his Brylcreem to make himself a little more presentable.

'It's okay, Henry. Really,' she whispered back, and genuinely smiled. 'Let's talk more when I get out of here.' She touched the side of his face, and Henry agreed.

Geraldine had lost touch with her brother, Henry, after Eileen's funeral, as everyone struggled to cope in their own way. Geraldine had thrown herself back into her work, and Henry had continued the family trait of propping up a bar, trying to forget the life he'd been born into. On his sixth birthday, he'd enquired as to where his mother was. He'd never asked the question before, and boldly stated, after blowing out the candles on his cake, that all his friends had mothers, so where was his. An awkward silence filled the room, the party guests looking to William. Playing a straight bat, he'd stated that she had gone to heaven when he was born, and when the angels took her, they left him as a gift. There were a few mutters and whispers around the room. Someone patted him on the back and stated how eloquently put his statement had been. Geraldine remembered how unimpressed Henry had seemed, and deep down, she believed he drank to fill the void of never knowing who his mother was or being able to feel and respond to the unique love shared between a mother and her child.

* * *

Two nights later, the evening before she was due to be discharged, Geraldine awoke in pain after unconsciously scratching at the wound site during her sleep. Flicking on her bedside light, she threw back the bed clothes, unceremoniously. To her horror she saw a translucent blue flame emanating from the wound site. Unable to move much, for fear of rupturing the staples holding the wound together, she shrieked.

The night nurse scurried to the room in time to see the unimaginable.

Geraldine was screaming and frantically thrashing at the bed clothes, which were engulfed in flames. It took the stunned nurse a moment to react before she slammed her palm against the fire alarm on the wall in the corridor and then scrambled a few metres further down the hallway to the fire extinguisher. She yanked it off the wall, lost her balance and stumbled. With no time to lose, she regained her composure, retrieved the extinguisher, which had slid across the floor, and doused Geraldine and her surroundings with the watery foam-like substance.

As fire fighters rushed to the horrific scene, it became too much for the nurse, who, upon looking at the now-silent Geraldine, collapsed into the arms of a hospital security guard.

Geraldine Ellis-Baxter was declared dead moments later.

This time there was a witness.

Chapter Sixteen

Heartache

At a quarter past midnight, William stirred from a deep sleep. When he registered the phone ringing, he threw back the bed covers, placed his feet into his slippers and reached for his dressing gown. In his drowsy state he muttered, 'Oh God, no. This better not be bad news.'

His heart sank when he answered. The Matron at the Louisville County Hospital was on the other end of the line. Geraldine had died and he needed to attend the hospital immediately. Claymore had already been called, and the Matron informed William that he would collect him on the way to the hospital. William felt instant constriction in his chest, like a knife had been plunged through his heart, the pain of anguish so intense he could hardly move. The loss of Eileen just two years prior was still raw.

The Matron's voice sounded distant on the line, like an echo, but after a moment, William indicated he understood and hung up. He sat there in the cold and dimly lit hallway, dumbstruck and numb. He gasped for air. He hadn't realised he'd stopped breathing when the Matron delivered the devastating news. The only sound he could hear was that of the old grandfather clock at the end of the hall: the unique creak, the pendulum made as it rocked back and forth, followed by a little click as the minute hand moved another notch on the cogged wheel. It was strangely hypnotic.

* * *

Fifteen minutes passed before Claymore knocked loudly on the front door. Tears had been streaming down his face. He could see a hall light on, but there was no answer. He knocked again and this time called out.

'William, it's Claymore.'

He peered through the glass panel on the front door. He could see William sitting by the phone, still in his striped, flan-nelette pyjamas and dressing gown. He knocked once more, and it jolted William out of his suspended state. Inching his way to the door, he grabbed his coat from the hat stand as he passed. Once he'd opened the door he embraced Claymore. Without saying a word, the tears flowed.

An hour passed before William and Claymore entered the hospital foyer, just after 1 a.m. Both men were ashen-faced, as they were escorted to the morgue where Geraldine had been moved while police combed the fire-damaged hospital room for evidence. The long, grey corridor seemed endless as the two men shuffled along. Reaching the end, they arrived at an ominous black door. The orderly then left. William took a deep breath and as he reached for the handle, he hesitated. Claymore, though equally distressed, took the lead and opened it.

The room was cold and dim, with only a single lamp illu-minating a desk covered in paperwork. They were met by the short, plump, balding mortician who introduced himself only as Roger, while the limp cigarette hanging from the corner of his mouth continually dropped ash on the floor.

Roger led Claymore and William to a wall with nine doors, stopping in front of the middle door on the middle row. It sounded like a fridge opening when the handle was released from its catch. A large metal trolley rolled out with Geraldine's remains covered by a white sheet. The mortician turned on a bright overhead light and proceeded to pull the sheet down to chest level. The body had been badly burned, and initially neither man could be certain of identity. The mortician presented the men with a small box. Inside were Geraldine's engagement and wedding rings, as well as other personal items from her hospital room, confirming the body as being hers.

William took a couple of steps closer. He felt his knees could go from under him at any moment and reached out to grab hold of the trolley. The ache in his chest, the lump in his throat and tears in his eyes were nearly too much. Instinctively, he reached out to touch her.

'I wouldn't do that, Sir.'

The mortician re-covered the remains and offered his condolences without a hint of empathy. She was then returned to her stainless-steel tomb. After positively identifying her, William and Claymore made their way from the morgue to the cafeteria to await further information from the authorities. Neither was hungry, and they barely spoke, but both were thinking of the immense suffering Geraldine must have endured in the final moments of her life.

* * *

Dr Strickland was excited, upon being informed by the police, there was a witness to the incident, other than the night nurse who'd attended to extinguish the blaze. A storage area adjacent to the fire-affected room was set up as an interview space.

Dr Strickland entered and set himself up at a large white desk upon which stood a phone and a lamp. In the corner was a filing cabinet, and behind the door was a hat stand awaiting its first item of clothing. A nurse presented at the door and assisted the witness inside.

'Hello. I'm Dr Strickland, the forensic pathologist.'

'Hello doctor. I'm Enid Crowhurst.' She gingerly shook his hand and proceeded to sit.

'I understand you were sharing the room across the hall with Geraldine Ellis-Baxter. Can you tell me what happened this evening?'

'Well, as I told the police, she was asleep when I returned from my bath at about ten. I recently had a hip operation and need to be able to move around on my own before they'll let me go home. I'm seventy-two, Dr Strickland, and I really like the food in here –.'

'That's nice, Enid. Please continue to tell me about Geraldine.'

'Yes. Right. Sorry. I like to read for a while before turning out the light. About half an hour passed and I could hear some moaning and groaning coming from her as she moved around in the bed. It's not uncommon to be uncomfortable after surgery, so I didn't think anything else much about it. I awoke when I heard her cry out, and noticed her bed light on. I saw what looked like a blue flame under her bedsheet as she kicked it up in the air. No sooner had she done that, flames engulfed her and shortly afterward the night nurse rushed in through the doorway.'

'Did the night nurse see you or say anything to you specifically?'

'No. I don't believe she saw me as I had gotten out of bed, grabbing my blanket to put over my head as I attempted to crawl to the water closet. I knew there was nothing I could do to help as I'm not physically strong enough to lift anything or have anyone lean on me. Before I could move further, the night nurse came back in with the fire extinguisher and put out the fire. That poor woman. The screaming, the panic, the smell ...'

'Is there anything else you can recall, Enid, that you think might be important?' Dr Strickland pressed.

'Well, now that you mention it, I could have sworn I saw a woman dressed in a long black gown standing in the doorway of our room just before the fire broke out.'

'You mean the night nurse?'

'No. All nurses here wear a light-blue and white knee-length outfit and a white cap. This woman had long black hair, unkept, and wore a black floor-length gown. I saw her just prior to Geraldine kicking the sheet in the air, which blocked my view of the door temporarily, and when the sheet came back down again, fully alight, she was gone. An instant later the nurse showed,' Enid said confidently.

'It sounds like you saw a nun. They visit the hospital frequently.'

'Possibly. However, nun's usually have their hair completely hidden by their habit.'

'So, you hadn't seen this woman before? Could she have been a family member visiting Geraldine, perhaps?'

'No, I hadn't seen her before, and I don't think so. All Geraldine's immediate family visited two days ago, and they were all men. Besides, visiting hours are strictly seven till nine.'

'Thank you, Enid. That's all for the moment. You have been most helpful.'

A nurse assisted Enid to her feet and out of the room as Dr Strickland left and made his way to the Matron's station, to see the guest register of those who had visited Geraldine that day. He also requested to speak with the operating surgeon as soon as he was available.

* * *

In the cafeteria, William was inconsolable. Losing his sister and two daughters under eerily similar circumstances made him angry and he wanted answers, only he had no idea of who to be angry at or where to start looking for them. His son, Henry, was thirty and he wondered if he too would die tragically at the age of thirty-four. It was no secret to anyone that he too had issues with alcohol. It was more than he could bare thinking about. Why thirty-four? What was the significance of that number and why his family? The early hour, lack of sleep and heightened emotions had taken its toll. He located a sofa in the corner and attempted to close his eyes.

* * *

The operating surgeon made his way to the interview room where Dr Strickland was waiting.

'Thank you for coming, Dr Stenholm. I'm sorry for calling you at this late hour. Please take a seat. I understand you operated on Geraldine Ellis-Baxter two days ago – abdominal surgery for a cyst on the liver?'

'That's right. There were no apparent issues post-surgery.'

'I see. A witness in the bed next to Geraldine reported seeing a blue flame appear from her abdominal region just prior to the outbreak of the fire. Would you know of any reason why that might be?'

'What do I look like, a fire investigator? Are you accusing me of something, Dr Strickland? How the hell would I know? Perhaps she was a smoker and the blue flame was from a cigarette lighter?'

The question, combined with a long double shift, and the late hour had worn his patience thin.

'No accusation, Dr Stenholm. I'm just after your professional opinion, or a possible explanation as to what might have caused the fire. The autopsy will shed further light on the subject. According to what I know from the family, Geraldine didn't smoke.'

'Very well. I apologise for my outburst. I guess it's possible the ethanol swabs used to sterilise the site, combined with the anaesthetic, could cause a chemical reaction resulting in spontaneous … But if so, it would be a first in my twenty-five-year career as a surgeon.'

'Thank you for your candour, Dr Stenholm. I'll let you know if I have further questions for you once I conduct the autopsy.'

'You do that. May I go home now?'

Dr Strickland motioned towards the door, and Dr Stenholm left.

Strickland knew he was in for a long night, and despite the late hour, he suspected he had another case of spontaneous human combustion on his hands, as Dr Stenholm had eluded. A review of the guest register earlier failed to corroborate Enid's account of a woman in black. The only visitors Geraldine had had were her father, brother and husband. As such, it wasn't enough to go to the police about. The only other person who could confirm Enid's account was the night nurse who'd put out the fire, but she was too traumatised to be interviewed and had been medicated.

After several hours conducting the autopsy, Dr Strickland had an initial summary of events. Geraldine had been a healthy young woman, other than the moderate case of Candida Albicans noted in her medical records. The autopsy did uncover medical negligence, as two ethanol swabs were left in her wound when it was stapled, though these had, most likely only caused some irritation as they hadn't yet become infected. PH levels of surviving tissue samples contradicted more than what would be considered normal in a healthy human being, as did potassium carbonate levels. Most of the corpse was a pile of ash, which is typically alkaline in nature, but the level of potassium carbonate could not be accurately measured due to the use of the fire extinguisher. He concluded the ethanol from the swabs, in combination with the anaesthetic, post-operative intravenous drugs and her gastrointestinal tract yeast infection, caused a spontaneous reaction to occur internally. The extensive damage to her internal organs around the operation site led him to conclude she had been burning internally long before the flame surfaced. Once it did, the rush of oxygen making contact with the flame ignited the bed sheet, and Geraldine, incapacitated from surgery, didn't stand a chance even with the quick actions of the night nurse.

He was clutching at straws to make the forensic and medical pieces fit together, as he had done with the previous family cases. He knew full well it wasn't just sheer coincidence three women from the same family had suffered the same fate at the same age.

Dr Strickland was alerted to the fact that William Ellis and Claymore Baxter were in the hospital cafeteria, and he went to speak with them. It was just after four-thirty.

Both men were dozing on the sofa when he entered. Dr Strickland extended his hand to Claymore, offering his condolences, and then said to William, 'There are no words.'

William put his hand on the doctor's shoulder before taking his seat again.

After a moment of silence, William turned to Dr Strickland and said, 'This isn't coincidence. I refuse to believe this happened naturally or innocently to our family three times. Something else has to be going on here and I'm asking for your help getting to the bottom of it. The police will think I'm just a crazy old man, and I know they're as frustrated as I am with two —, soon to be three — unsolved cases concerning this family. It's bad enough not having definitive answers as to why your loved ones are no longer here, but it's worse being judged by the entire community. The whispers, the rumours. I need it to stop.'

Dr Strickland knew William well enough to know he was serious and it wasn't just the ramblings of a mentally exhausted, grief-stricken man.

'I happen to agree with you, William, and I will do my best to find out why and how this was possible. I'll leave no stone unturned to find an acceptable answer for you, however long it takes.'

'Thank you, Dr Strickland. We appreciate whatever you can find out. The whispers we hear around the place about our family being cursed were hard to take initially, but I'm inclined to believe them now,' Claymore added, as he and William stood to leave.

Dr Strickland looked at his watch. Five am. Fighting his tiredness, he decided to review the Ellis cases. There was clearly a connection. All three women were from the one family and all had died at the age of thirty-four from a fire-related event. Was something spiritual going on? Was it a curse of some kind, as Claymore Baxter had indicated? Was the woman dressed in black connected to the family in some way? If he could join the dots, he believed it would be the first ever documented case of a family connection of Spontaneous Human Combustion. Too many questions and too few answers. But he was struggling to keep his eyes open. Further investigation would have to wait until after he'd slept.

Chapter Seventeen

Cursed

A gain, Dr Strickland had the unenviable task of delivering an autopsy report to the Ellis family. This time, he would make a house call and hand it to William and Claymore in person.

Two days later, he knocked on William's front door. Soon after, he heard heavy and deliberate footsteps approaching.

'Come in, Marcus.' William shook his hand and proceeded to take his coat.

'Thank you, William. It's good to see you; albeit, I wish it could be under better circumstances.' Dr Strickland made his way into the kitchen where Claymore was already seated with coffee in hand.

'Hello Claymore.'

'Hello Dr Strickland.' Claymore stood and shook his hand.

Dr Strickland dug into his leather satchel to retrieve the report, and handed copies to the men.

'William and Claymore, as you know, my findings into Geraldine's death is again SHC. At the hospital, you asked me to do some digging into why this was happening to the women in your family, and I have begun that task earnestly.

* * *

One week later …

Claymore Baxter loved to spoil his wife, something his position at Chevrolet allowed. No expense would be spared when it came to her funeral. Thankfully, Geraldine had been a great organiser and had filed all the details of her sister's funeral, which she'd arranged a few years prior, so he could use this information as his baseline. The number of mourners would likely be extensive, as Geraldine was well liked and respected at both Pierre Cardin and Chevrolet. Father Pritchard would preside over the funeral, and her casket would be identical to Eileen's, except it would be overflowing with carnations: her favourite flower. Psalm 23 would be read, but instead of 'Amazing Grace', the hymn 'How Great Thou Art' would be performed by the local church choir as it was her favourite hymn.

The day of the funeral arrived, and the local Catholic church filled to capacity as people gathered to pay their respects. Tomas escorted William into the church via a private side entrance. He was again heavily medicated, and this time wheelchair bound, as the weight of loss on his shoulders was too much for his middle-aged legs to bear. Josephine obediently followed closely behind and waited patiently for Tomas to instruct her where to sit. As he did so, she tugged at his pants and indicated she would rather sit next to grandpa, which was directly in front of the casket.

Father Pritchard began his sombre welcome as a sea of gloomy faces stared back at him. Psalm 23 was then read by Claymore's best friend, before the choir performed a hauntingly beautiful version of 'How Great Thou Art'. As the last note was sung, the heavens chimed in with a loud clap of thunder, causing a couple of pigeons to coo and relocate in the rafters. An invitation was made to mourners to speak if they wished. A steady stream of people made their way to the front, some with only a few well-chosen words, others with stories of shopping trips or product launches that had gone awry in the past. Claymore was the last to speak.

'My beautiful wife, the irrepressible and irreplaceable Geraldine, has left us. I first met her at a Chevrolet conference, when Pierre Cardin were having their annual sales conference at the same venue in Houston, Texas, approximately ten years ago. I saw her at the bar —, beautiful blonde hair, silk scarf around her neck, soft pink bolero cardigan and dark-coloured slacks. I offered to buy her a drink and we got chatting. She had style, poise and grace. I knew after our first meeting I wanted to make her my wife. I recall her unrepressed joy at becoming an aunty to Josephine, as we couldn't have children of our own. She was a workaholic and, as such, regularly achieved saleswoman of the month awards. She loved the travel and the networking her job afforded. My life, and that of her family, was richer for having known her. She has gone ahead of us to be reunited with her mother, Bernadette, her Aunty Margaret and her sister, Eileen. I miss you more than words can accurately express. Rest in peace, my darling.'

At the conclusion of the service, an invitation was made to gather at the cemetery for the committal of the body to the earth. The weather hadn't improved, and it was now steadily raining as mourners made their way out the church to the cemetery, down the road. As the casket was lowered to its final resting place alongside Bernadette, Margaret and Eileen, William scanned the crowd through hazy eyes, struggling to focus. His view became crystal clear, however, when he saw the same woman dressed in black from Eileen's funeral. She was looking straight at him when their eyes met.

'Hey! Hey you! Yes, you in the black,' William shouted, his boney finger pointed in her direction.

The mourners turned and parted to see who William was talking about, and someone standing nearby whispered, 'There's nobody there.'

'I can see you. Who are you? Nobody seems to know who you are, yet you turn up to both my daughters' funerals. Why?' William exclaimed, as he struggled with his wheelchair, eager to get across to her.

The priest continued, fully aware of how grief can affect emotions, as Tomas tried to restrain and calm William.

'Can't you see her, Tomas? It's pouring with rain. She has no umbrella, yet she isn't getting wet. Can't you see her?' William pleaded, before slumping in his chair, exhausted.

* * *

For most of his career, Dr Marcus Strickland had been able to provide conclusions, and subsequently peace of mind, to loved ones for each case he took on. He'd previously had no need to scratch the itch of curiosity, because his findings had been a neatly packaged parcel wrapped in certainty and tied up with scientific explanation. That was, until he met William Ellis and his family. At William and Claymore's insistence, Dr Strickland had stepped outside his scientific mindset and training, because the itch had developed into a rash and it was time to broaden his way of thinking. He began researching the Ellis family tree at the state library archives, using census data and cross-referencing court records of births, deaths and marriages. He was looking for any patterns involving deaths relating to fire, particularly among women.

After many painstaking hours flicking through old and dusty, faded ledgers, and surviving parish medical records, he discovered that cases of Spontaneous Human Combustion had begun, with the daughter of the Chief Judge John Winthrop Ellis in 1703. Clemantyne was thirty-four, her death was recorded as being caused by a lightning strike during a family outing, though the weather was clear, and witnesses saw no lightning or heard any residual thunder. The hand-written statement, given by her mother, and recorded by the local parish sheriff, was a sensational and difficult read. Partly because it was quite faded, but also because of the content and archaic language. In part, it said:

The family was taking a stroll through a park on the edge of town. Clemantyne was talking to her mother about a young man she'd met at the local market the day before when she suddenly fell silent mid-sentence. Georgette, Clemantyne's mother, turned to look at her and noticed nothing out of the ordinary, except as she leant in to touch her, Clemantyne was enveloped in blue flame. The intensity of the heat forced Georgette to back away, and she screamed for her husband to fetch water from the nearby river. By the time he returned, Clemantyne had disintegrated into a pile of ash and the blue flame had vanished. She didn't appear distressed or panicked. For someone who was apparently on fire, her clothes and skin didn't appear to burn.

John Winthrop Ellis was the chief judge overseeing the Salem Witch Trials when Constance Martinez was accused, convicted and burned at the stake for being a witch in 1692. The public records noted that she cursed him, saying that every female born of his line would suffer at the hands of fire in their third decade of life. It was also noted that it took the court just thirty-four minutes to find Constance Martinez guilty of the crime she was accused of. Margaret, Eileen and Geraldine had all been thirty-four when they died mysteriously at the hands of fire, and all were direct descendants of his line. Following the seemingly logical pieces of this cursed puzzle suggested Josephine, Eileen's daughter, would also suffer from a fiery event if and when she reached that age, as well as any female children she might have in the future.

The hair on the back of Dr Strickland's neck rose when we saw a hand drawn image of Constance Martinez, as depicted on the day she'd died — long black hair and, a long black gown. Was she the woman Enid saw standing in the doorway? It was scarcely believable.

What the hell am I supposed to do with this information? Who would believe me?

In all his years of investigating and unravelling many forensic findings, Dr Strickland's most intriguing and interesting work had been centred around the Ellis family. The surviving family members needed closure, and for future cases of SHC, it had to be documented fully and factually. It didn't matter whether the medical and/or legal establishments shunned the findings, or if they requested he surrender his medical licence due to some perceived cognitive decline, as his retirement was forthcoming. The only person who needed the information was William Ellis. William had to be told that his granddaughter would be another victim.

After six hours of reading, making notes and ingesting information, Dr Strickland needed to stretch his legs, rest his eyes and consume a large cup of coffee. He made his way up the stairs and knocked on the door to exit the secure room for ten minutes.

Upon his return, the door was unlocked by the attendant, who asked him to surrender the remainder of his coffee in accordance with the signage on the door stating liquids were not permitted in the viewing room. He then descended the stairs and was astonished to discover the space in complete disarray. Most of the fragile papers were scattered all over the floor, as if someone had swept them off the desk. The table itself, along with the chair in which he'd been sitting, were both on their side. No-one else was around, and he was the only one to have booked the space for the day.

There was a feeling of unease in the air as he carefully re-constructed the space, retrieved the debris and recommenced collating and marking the statements, medical records and pictures he wanted copied. He sensed he was being watched. Not by a suspicious librarian who was concerned at someone making too much noise, but by someone or something darker in nature. The hairs on the back of his neck and on his forearms slowly rose. He decided to step out on a limb.

'Constance? Are you here?' he asked, looking around the room for any sign of a reply — a flicker of light, independent movement of paperwork. But there was nothing. 'I want to let you know, I'm not a threat. I'm simply trying to understand and help a friend.'

Still nothing.

'Don't be silly, Marcus. There's no-one else here,' he muttered under his breath.

In the farthest corner of the room, down the end of an aisle, Constance had a direct line of sight on Dr Strickland. She chose to remain hidden, because she knew his words were true, and nothing he had discovered would threaten the course of her vengeance.

* * *

Sixteen years later ...

It had taken the long-since retired Dr Strickland several attempts to explain his lengthy findings to William, particularly when he referred to the Ellis family deaths as being linked to a curse.

Initially, William thought Dr Strickland had lost his

mind when he first heard the outrageous suggestion, several months after he received Geraldine's autopsy report, but Dr Strickland persisted. William had asked him to uncover the truth, however hard it might be to swallow, and years later he eventually thanked his old friend for doing so. It had given him a sense of closure that had long eluded him.

In addition to the information he had imparted to William, Dr Strickland took up a new vocation in retirement and committed many painstaking hours to spontaneous human combustion research. He felt the community needed to know about the lives of those who'd suffered SHC, and that our understanding of the basic principles of physics needed to be broadened. So, the compilation of his book began. He'd never heard former colleagues refer to SHC or mention any cases over the years. He sensed there was a 'don't ask, don't tell' mentality. He knew his own reputation was under threat as a result of the triplicate Ellis family findings.

Over the last five hundred years, there had been hundreds of instances of SHC throughout America and France, across to England, Scotland, even India and South Australia. The causes of death were rarely recorded as SHC. More often it was death by burning, unknown causes, death by misadventure or accidental death. However, the psychological and evidentiary profile of the victims Dr Strickland had researched, formed an elite SHC group of unfortunates.

Despite all the training and medical expertise he had under his belt, this contentious and essentially banished phenomena interested and fascinated him the most. His book,

'*The Hidden Fire*,' had been published and had, as expected, received mixed reviews. Many mistook it as a work of fiction, rather than a factual account. Former colleagues and fellow scientists completely dismissed it, stating it had no bearing on reality, ridiculing him whilst they distanced themselves. It did gain interest with other believers, though, who made him aware of other cases from around the world, giving him enough material for a second book if he so desired.

* * *

You could have forgiven William for thinking the worst life had to dish out was behind him. However, death wasn't finished with him and his family just yet.

For a time, Henry, Tomas and Hosea worked the family ranch as the painful loss of the women in their lives somewhat abated. From many years of hard drinking, the damage finally caught up with Henry and he'd been diagnosed with cirrhosis. Doctors informed him that unless a compatible donor liver became available within months, it would be all the time he had left. Instead of forcing an about-face change to his daily routine, the news sent him spiralling further downward.

One day, without saying a word to anyone, he took the shotgun from its storage locker in the stock shed and drove up to the top paddock. He parked the truck a short distance from a large oak tree and tied the shotgun to the front grill, attaching the remaining rope to the trigger. Then sat at the base of the tree and consumed a large bottle of vodka. He looked out across the land and realised, he'd never truly appreciated the beauty of it.

After consuming the last drop of alcohol, he launched the bottle towards a nearby rock, where it smashed, and yanked the rope. His self-loathing, loveless life was over. He was just forty-five, and the year was 1981.

William had tried over the years to connect with Henry on his level, even encouraged him to see a GP to get some help. Henry was wired differently, and William believed the lack of a mother-figure in his life had greatly affected his ability to nurture and connect with others. Henry searched in vain for comfort, and when it all got too hard, he would turn to drink to switch off from life.

Tomas had heard the shot from the house and figured it came from his neighbour's place up the hill. It was only when Henry didn't return for dinner that night that he went looking. William had approached Father Pritchard about conducting the funeral service, but the church didn't condone suicide. He also discovered Henry wouldn't be buried on consecrated ground in the church cemetery. Father Pritchard explained he wasn't taking the position to be hurtful, but that it was the church's position, and as a priest he needed to abide by it. William understood, and after discussion with Tomas, Henry's funeral was planned as a private family affair with a lay preacher presiding. Henry was buried at the spot where he took his own life and a plaque was attached to the rock nearby.

After Henry's death, Tomas and Hosea continued with

the ranch for a short while, but their passion for it had died with him and they eventually put it up for sale. Over the years, several local ranchers, and a couple from out of state, had approached Tomas to sell, but he'd always resisted. He'd wanted Josephine to have a familiar place to call home, should her own career ambitions not work out.

With part of the proceeds from the sale of the ranch, Tomas decided to take a risk and invest in emerging mobile telephone technologies. He could see the benefits of being more connected, and the potential increase in productivity as a result. He wanted to invest the remainder of the funds in another worthwhile cause, and reward an individual for his loyalty throughout the years. He gave Hosea fifty percent, and thanked him for all his years of service. It was the single most generous act of gratitude Hosea had ever received and it would change his life.

With the rights of African-American citizens being more freely recognised, and some of those citizens being elected into positions of authority, Hosea used the funds to purchase a place of his own in Louisville. He enrolled at The University of Alabama to take a degree in political science, and upon graduation, he worked his way up through the business community.

When the local government called for candidates to nominate for Governor of Alabama, family acquaintances came from every direction to support Hosea. Whilst the team surrounding his parents had been forced to disband when they died, a few had kept tabs on his movements over the years, and they deemed it time. It proved to be divine, as he was elected, unopposed, as the first African-American Governor of Alabama.

Chapter Eighteen

Josephine

J osephine had never liked school. She always complained there were not enough opportunities to be creative, and she hated math and science as she didn't understand them. Two subjects, however, that did capture her attention were geography and world history. She wanted to travel and see the world she only understood existed in picture books. Tomas put in many hours of extra tutoring, as work on the ranch allowed, but her focus was on being creative, and school restricted her ability to do that.

Once she turned sixteen, Tomas allowed her to leave school and assist him on the ranch, as well as working part-time at the local corner store. He saw it as a way of continuing her education, as she would learn life skills ahead of her peers, having initially been behind in life due to her late mother's choices. She also followed in Eileen's footsteps in being able to turn trash into treasure, and the ranch provided many opportunities to find that special piece and repurpose it. Meanwhile, working at the corner store allowed her to save some money, so that one day she could realise her dream of travelling abroad. The store even agreed to sell some of her recreations on consignment, and for a time she struggled to keep up with demand. Tomas was pleased with her initiative and often assisted with tasks that required more expertise, such as welding, metal cutting and concreting.

The spring of 1976 was particularly harsh — unusually wet and cold. Typically, orphaned calves would not survive without human intervention, and Josephine had expressed an interest in the cattle in recent times. So, the family of two became five, with regular bottle feeding of three calves. Two were orphaned and the other one half of a twinned pair, rejected by its mother because it was the weakest.

Josephine was initially apprehensive as three, seventy-pound, gangly calves jumped about her with boundless energy. Tomas showed her how to interact with the calves safely and feed them. Initially the feeding routine of 250ml five times a day, took some getting used to. Many bumps, bruises and trodden-on toes were endured as animal and human jostled for position. Eventually, Josephine gained confidence and as the weeks went by, mutual trust developed. At nine months of age, Boss, Lulu and Toey, as Josephine had called them, each weighing in at six-hundred pounds, had been weaned and followed her around everywhere. They would see her coming toward the fence at feeding time and made their way to her before she'd even had a chance to call their names. Tomas was proud of Josephine's confidence and independence. She'd shown reliability and dedication to farming procedures and safety around animals and hadn't been afraid to ask questions when clarification was required.

By the time she was thirty, she'd travelled through and seen over a dozen different countries outside of America and had lived in both Spain and Brazil. She chose Spain because she'd lived with and loved cattle her entire life, and she was drawn to seeing them wander through a historic city rather than the confines of a paddock.

Having moved to Pamplona, Spain in July 1985, she'd settled into her rented apartment shortly before the Feast of St Fermin Festival. One day, as streets began to close off for the route the bulls would run, Josephine was outside of a protected spectator area. When several bulls thundered toward her, she felt a hand on the back of her neck as someone pulled her backwards, out of harm's way. Ancient dust fell from the building facade above her as she landed heavily on the cobblestone street. Momentarily stunned by the force of being dragged backwards, she finally sat up to thank the person who had saved her, only there was no-one there. A few stunned faces — people who'd seen the miraculous backward jump —, stared at her from behind protective barriers and balconies, all well out of reach. Not being an overly religious person, she thanked the angels for protection under as she picked herself up and dusted herself off, but the message wouldn't reach them because Constance stepped in to claim it.

Josephine loved the atmosphere of the week-long festivities and tried to immerse herself in as much of it as she could. It felt like one big party, with music, dancing, street entertainers, parades and fireworks. Visually, Pamplona was spectacular, many baroque, neoclassical and gothic buildings providing a stunning backdrop for the events taking place. Grand residences were opened to the public for guided tours, which Josephine took advantage of. Having grown up in a modest homestead made entirely of wood, she couldn't help but feel a little envious of the wealth some people had to build such huge, solid, decretive buildings out of stone.

By the time she was thirty-two, an opportunity arose for Josephine to travel to Brazil. Some friends she'd gotten to know in Spain were heading to the Carnival in Rio de Janeiro, which was something she'd learned about in history class and one day hoped she'd see. If you didn't dress up, down or inside out you would appear out of place, so her friends encouraged her to go on a shopping spree for an outfit she wouldn't otherwise have dreamed of wearing. With costumes purchased, it was time to begin the next adventure and board a plane.

It was the longest flight she'd taken, over eight hours in the air before they landed at Galeao International Airport. During the flight, a handsome Brazilian, returning home from holidays, kept looking and smiling at her from the row across the aisle. She wasn't sure how to interpret his behaviour until one of her friends noticed and told her he fancied her. Josephine was relatively inexperienced when it came to men, having only had one relationship for a few brief months with a local boy from Louisville before she left to commence her travels.

As everyone exited the plane and made their way to collect their bags, Josephine dropped a magazine she'd been reading. The man who'd been interested in her during the flight picked it up and pursued her, waiting for the right moment to introduce himself. As he arrived at the baggage carousel, he walked up and stood alongside her.

'Hello, I'm Carlos Martinez, and I think you dropped this back there.'

His accent alone was enough to get Josephine flustered, and she could feel herself beginning to melt, like butter on a hot day.

'Oh, did I? Thank you, Carlos. I'm Josephine Ellis.' She smiled as she took the magazine from his warm hand, noticing a wedding ring.

As quickly as the flustered feelings rose, they died away again. After all, a handsome, tall, tanned, brown-eyed, smartly dressed, man couldn't possibly have been single.

'Are you here for Carnival?' Carlos enquired, knowing she'd seen his ring.

'Yes, I am actually. With some friends I met in Spain. It's our first.'

'Then I simply must show you around. As a local, it's tradition, and I insist.' Carlos said, with a genuine sense of pride.

Her friends had overheard the comment and rushed over, ecstatic they now had a local tour guide. Apprehensively, Josephine agreed, and they all piled into a taxi.

'Do you know much about Carnival?' Carlos asked as they travelled to the girls' hotel at Copacabana Beach.

One of Josephine's encyclopaedic friends rattled off the history as everyone intently listened.

'Yes, that's how it began, but these days it's about pretending to be someone or something else. You surrender yourself to the music, the atmosphere and let go of who you are for a short while as you live out a fantasy.'

The temperature quickly rose inside the taxi, and the flustered feelings experienced earlier returned. Josephine and Carlos shared another moment of eye contact, followed by a shy smile.

'Is it hot in here or is it just him?' The taxi driver campily said, as he wound down his window and the vehicle filled with cooler air and laughter.

The girls quickly learned that at this time of the year anything goes, and you just go with the flow and get back to worrying about your life afterwards. For Josephine, the experience would change the direction of her life forever.

Chapter Nineteen

Sage Advice

William never regarded himself as a religious man, in any sense of the word. He had confided in Father Dominic Pritchard, when his sister was tragically taken many decades earlier, and then again after the funerals of both of his daughters and only son. He otherwise chose to steer clear of the 'politics of the place' as he referred to it. The time had come, however, for another frank chat as the issue for discussion weighed heavily on his ageing conscience.

Using a walking stick, but still under his own steam, William made his way up the church steps, possibly for the last time, and shook the hand of the slightly built, beautiful young woman who was greeting parishioners as they entered. The Louisville Catholic church was the oldest in the state, with the largest number of stained-glass windows per square meter. For the first time, he noticed the ornate beauty of the building. He took a seat near the confessional box while he plucked up his courage.

After several moments, he entered, closing the door behind him before Father Pritchard slid the privacy screen across. William began by making a sign of the cross and said, 'Forgive me, Father, for it has been many, many years since my last confession.' His voice broke slightly under the emotion of the questions to come.

Father Pritchard responded, 'Please continue, my son.'

'Father, is it considered a mortal sin to humanely kill someone in order to save them from another horrible death?'

It seemed like an eternity before, Father Pritchard spoke. 'Our Lord God tells us in the book of Exodus, chapter twenty verse thirteen, thou shalt not kill, regardless of the reason behind the act.'

'Okay, I understand, but doesn't the Bible also state that people have a right to defend themselves against attack and use deadly force if necessary?'

'Yes it does, with an example in the book of Esther, chapter eight verses ten and eleven. This is different to premeditated murder, however.' Father Pritchard made the distinction clear.

William thought for a moment and then said, 'I'm an old man, Father. I'm tired and weary of life and feel my end days are near. I want to ensure that, when I'm gone, my remaining family has the opportunity to live without fear. Thank you for your time, Father. You have provided me with some much needed clarity.'

'Bless you my son. May you live out the rest of your days free and blameless in His eyes.'

Father Pritchard knew the voice on the other side of the confessional box. He, too, was getting weary, and his heart ached for William and what he'd had to endure over the years.

As William exited the confessional, a ray of light shone at his feet from the large stained-glass window to his left above the altar. He took it as a sign, and smiled as he slowly made his way out the church and down the front steps. A sense of peace came over him. He knew what he needed to do to free his family from a three-hundred-year-old curse. The veil had been lifted, and the haze of grief he had been living under for the best part of his adult life evaporated.

Josephine was now thirty-three, and William was about to turn ninety.

Josephine was due to visit early the following day. They hadn't seen each other in six months, as she'd been travelling in Brazil, but she'd mentioned on the phone she had some exciting news to share with him.

On his way home from church, a quick stop at the local drug store was in order. During the evening meal he'd add sleeping pills to her food, and when she became tired, he'd assist her to bed, ensuring he positioned her face down into her pillow. The intent being she'd suffocate during the night, sparing her the agony of an untimely death by fire, and breaking the curse in the process. These thoughts ambled through his mind as he slowly drove home. It would be murder through compassionate necessity rather than malicious intent. At least this was what he told himself as he recalled the sage advice the priest had imparted.

A short distance from home, William saw a woman walking along the road. She was slightly stooped, dressed in a long black gown, with messy black hair. As he got closer, he thought she looked familiar, but he couldn't place her. He recalled the dossier of paperwork from Dr Strickland, in particular the hand-drawn image pinned to the cover, and he instantly connected the dots. However inconceivable it was, he believed the woman to be Constance Martinez, from the account of her appearance on the day of her death in 1692. He was convinced she was the same woman who had appeared at both his daughters' funerals, and in the hospital, right before the fire that claimed Geraldine's life. With no further time to think, and believing what he saw to be true, he sped up and didn't deviate from his path.

A second before impact, she turned, and when their eyes met, he knew the face to be that of his grand-daughter, Josephine. Her head penetrated the windscreen of the vehicle with a sickening crack, before her lifeless body was cast aside. The vehicle continued through the bridge's guard rail into the still waters of the river below.

Momentarily dazed as water gushed in, William consumed his last gasps of air, horrified at the course of action he'd chosen moments earlier and struck with pangs of guilt. Peering out the shattered windscreen, he noticed an image moving toward him from the riverbed. Struggling to release himself from the seatbelt that restrained him, he became further incapacitated by fear, as the water level rose higher.

The ghostly spirit of Constance Martinez hovered over the crushed bonnet of the vehicle, her head tilted to one side as she studied the frail, yet determined victim before her. During his lifetime he had endured more than most parents should have to, and in a way, Constance admired his resilience.

The last words William heard were: 'Did you think you could outsmart me? The grave didn't stop me. You couldn't stop me. Josephine is mine.'

As she entered the shattered windscreen and passed through the vehicle, William drowned.

A witness, who saw the car go through the railing, jumped into the river to assist, but by the time he reached the vehicle, it was clear there was nothing to be done. When ambulance and police arrived at the scene, Josephine Henrietta Hubbard was pronounced dead, but her unborn child still had a faint heartbeat. Time was now against the paramedics to keep blood circulating through Josephine's lifeless body as they made their way to hospital, if they were to save the baby's life. Tomas knew of the relationship his daughter had had with a married man, during her time abroad, but it was kept quiet from the rest of the family, as was her pregnancy. The family had endured more than most over the years, and a scandalous revelation would only stir up the rumour mill again.

Upon arrival at the hospital, a grief-stricken Tomas was pacing the waiting room, as he'd done thirty-three years earlier, only this time a different set of emotions gripped him. The giant pendulum of life and death was in motion. Would he be a grandfather, or would he be forced to plan a double funeral? His thoughts were interrupted by a knock on the waiting room door.

'Excuse me, are you Mr Tomas Hubbard?' a police officer enquired.

'Yes I am.'

'I'm so sorry for your loss. I understand the deceased was your daughter?'

'Yes, my pregnant daughter. Do you have any news of her baby?' Tomas pressed.

'No, I'm sorry, I don't. But I do have some other information for you. Please take a seat.' The police officer motioned in the direction of the nearest chair. 'It appears the vehicle that struck your daughter was being driven by a Mr William Ellis. Do you know that name?'

'William? Oh my God. Yes, that's her grandfather and my ex-father-in-law, but ... that can't be possible. Are you saying it was a ... hit and run?' Tomas spluttered.

'Not exactly. His vehicle was found at the scene, at the bottom of the riverbed, near the foundations of the bridge. Mr Ellis was still strapped into the driver's seat and is deceased. It's unclear at this time as to whether it was a deliberate act or purely an accident. There were no braking marks on the road. He may have suffered a medical episode at the wheel and couldn't avoid a collision. We are still investigating.'

Tomas was motionless and speechless, trying to digest the information as the officer continued to speak.

'Were you aware of any animosity between the two?'

Tomas was silent. He hadn't heard the question.

'Sir, were you aware of any animosity between them? the officer repeated.

'Sorry. Umm ... no, none whatsoever. They adored each other. He was an eighty-nine-year-old man. He was thrilled that his granddaughter wanted to include him in her life. We'd started planning his ninetieth birthday celebration for next month. She was going to share the news of her pregnancy with him then. They hadn't seen each other in some time, and now … they're both gone.' Tomas was shaking.

'Okay, Mr Hubbard. It appears it may have been a terrible accident, but we'll wait on an autopsy for cause of death to be established before we can let you know any more.' The officer shook Tomas' hand and left the waiting room.

Just then, a nurse entered the waiting room, and ushered Tomas to follow her. As they walked down the corridor, a shell-shocked Tomas could see her lips moving, but he couldn't hear a word she was saying. He stopped as his body and most of his senses had ground to a halt. The nurse continued momentarily, before realising something was wrong and returned to where Tomas had awkwardly propped himself up against the wall.

'Mr Hubbard? Mr Hubbard?' She gently shook his shoulder, unaware of the horrific news the police officer had relayed to him minutes earlier.

'Sorry. What?' Tomas replied, red-faced and wiping away tears.

'I was saying your daughter's child survived. You're a grand-father.' Her tone conveyed the bittersweet empathy of the situation.

As they rounded the corner to the nursery, he peered in through the viewing window. The nurse motioned to the midwife, who wheeled the humidicrib over. Tomas was a grandfather to a very lucky baby girl. As he tapped on the glass, trying to get the youngster's attention, it was clear something had captured her attention elsewhere. Tomas followed her gaze to the ceiling corner of the room, but saw nothing.

Unseen to all present, hovering above them, Constance Martinez stared back at the child as she grappled with mixed emotion. Her curse had been thwarted by a descendant's love. Something she hadn't foreseen. She had a decision to make – continue her centuries-long vengeance, after all she'd gotten used to the rush her wrath gave her, or fade quietly and contentedly into the background and give up the thirst that was never fully satisfied.

She just smiled back.

Acknowledgments

My eternal gratitude to Amy, Jessi, Deanne, Tia, Nicola and my partner Jason for taking the time to read and critique constructively along the way. The creative mind can take you off in many different directions – learning to harness and focus it to produce a cohesive story has been a challenge. I still have much to learn and hope that a lifetime of writing will provide me with a legacy to be proud of.